Windy Creek Stables
Presley and the Impossible Dream

Windy Creek Stables
Presley and the Impossible Dream

Kaitlyn Sage Patterson
with illustrations by Kelley McMorris

Feiwel and Friends

New York

A Feiwel and Friends Book
An imprint of Macmillan Publishing Group, LLC
120 Broadway, New York, NY 10271 • mackids.com

Text copyright © 2025 by Kaitlyn Sage Patterson. Illustrations copyright © 2025 by Kelley McMorris. Horseshoe illustration copyright © 2025 by AK_Vector / Shutterstock. Rope illustrations copyright © 2025 by Macrovector / Shutterstock. All rights reserved.

Our books may be purchased in bulk for promotional, educational, or business use. Please contact your local bookseller or the Macmillan Corporate and Premium Sales Department at (800) 221-7945 ext. 5442 or by email at MacmillanSpecialMarkets@macmillan.com.

Library of Congress Cataloging-in-Publication Data is available.

First edition, 2025
Book design by Trisha Previte
Feiwel and Friends logo designed by Filomena Tuosto
Printed in the United States of America by Lakeside Book Company, Harrisonburg, Virginia

ISBN 978-1-250-33135-9 (paperback)
10 9 8 7 6 5 4 3 2 1

ISBN 978-1-250-33136-6 (hardcover)
10 9 8 7 6 5 4 3 2 1

To my parents, for helping me follow my dreams

Windy Creek Stables
Presley and the Impossible Dream

Chapter One

Presley tapped her pencil's eraser against her chin, scowling at her English homework. Between the barking dogs, yowling cats, and the fact that she absolutely loathed diagramming sentences, she was pretty sure that she wasn't *actually* going to get any homework done until her stepdad's veterinary clinic closed for the day. In fact, she'd already reorganized the supply closet, inventoried the donation bins, and alphabetized the veterinary textbooks in her stepdad's office just to avoid her homework. And even though she'd have to tackle her English homework *eventually*, she decided that it would be way easier to concentrate on it at home. Not that Presley's house was much more peaceful than the office. Between her mom, stepdad, all of her siblings, and their ever-growing collection of pets, the Elder-Sharaf household was, at its best, a sort of loosely controlled chaos.

Presley's parents had been divorced for a long time, and their homes couldn't have been more different. She spent every other week at her dad and stepmom's neat, quiet house. They only had one pet, a poodle named Biscuit, who was as tidy and reserved as her owners. Presley loved the serenity and peace there.

But when Presley was at her mom and stepdad's house, she had an ally in her stepdad, Mahal, who loved animals almost as much as Presley. He'd have to—he was a vet. When Presley's mom agreed to marry Mahal, she made a "no more than eight furry legs in the house" rule. Unfortunately for her, both Presley and Mahal were extremely good at loopholes.

There were currently ten furry legs—a Maine Coon cat and a greyhound who only had three legs each and a hairless Sphynx cat named Bisous who Mom counted as furry even though he really didn't have much more than peach fuzz—eight scaly legs, a snake, and about fifteen birds—mostly chickens, quail, and pheasants—living in the Elder-Sharaf household. Presley had wheedled and begged and promised to take excellent care of each animal she'd convinced her mom to let her bring home.

Mom and Mahal may have had slightly different

ideas about how many pets was too many, but they agreed on one thing: When you have an animal, their needs come first. Presley cleaned up after each and every animal in their house, made sure they always had fresh food and water, kept their things neat and tidy, and ensured they were always well groomed.

Nowadays Mom just sighed and smiled whenever Presley and Mahal brought home a new pet, but she wouldn't budge on her "no horses" rule. She was terrified of horses, and she was dead set against Presley learning to ride. Presley had begged. She'd pleaded. She'd even made a whole presentation about the benefits of horsemanship for young people. She wanted to show her mom that she just *knew* that horses would understand her better than any person ever had. If she just had the chance, she could finally be seen for the real version of herself. Not the kid her parents and teachers saw, or the side of herself she showed her friends and classmates, but her truest self—the part of her that only a horse could bring out. The brave, dauntless, powerful version of Presley. But none of her presentations had quite managed to change her mom's mind. Not yet at least.

The office door squealed on its hinges and Dr. Peters,

her stepdad's business partner, poked his head in. "Hey, Presley," he said, smiling as he greeted her. "Have you seen Mahal?"

"I think he's finishing up with a yakking bulldog," Presley said, and grinning mischievously, added, "Or maybe it was a yak with a bullying problem?"

Dr. Peters guffawed, slapping a pale white hand against his starched khakis in a way that was both cringingly exaggerated and genuine at the same time. He'd always appreciated Presley's jokes, even before her mom had married Mahal, back when their animals were just patients at the vet practice. Now that Presley spent a couple hours at the office every day after school, she worked extra hard to make him laugh. When he was in an especially good mood, he'd let her watch procedures in the back and ask all the questions she could think of.

"When you see him, ask him if he's got time for a consult tonight with me?" Dr. Peters asked, checking his watch nervously. "I need to do a PPE, and my assistant is out sick."

Presley, who prided herself on remembering everything she could about the equine side of Dr. Peters's practice, blurted, "You mean a pre-purchase exam? For a horse? Can I help?"

Presley loved horses. She loved all animals, but horses were something special. Mahal indulged her fascination, slipping facts about animals into dinner conversation all the time. Just the other day he'd sent her down an evolutionary biology rabbit hole by mentioning that, like dogs and cats, horses evolved alongside humans, but they were different. For a long time, people had kept them around because they served a purpose.

But when Presley watched the top riders in the world compete in the dressage arena or on the cross-country field, she saw a true partnership. A person and an animal working together to make magic. She'd never pretended to be a wizard, a space explorer, or the president. Presley had always had one goal. She wanted to be an equestrian. She had wanted to learn to ride for as long as she could remember. And for longer than that, her mom had been dead set against the idea.

Dr. Peters, who could apparently tell Presley was starting to scheme from the look on her face, put up a hand to make her pause and said, "Hold up there, cowgirl. You're right. It's a pre-purchase exam for a horse over at Windy Creek Stables. The minute you get your vet tech license or your veterinary degree, you're hired and can help me with every PPE I do," he promised. "Until then, see if you can't catch your stepdad for me, okay?"

Presley nodded, excitement building despite Dr. Peters's cautions. She could almost smell the stables already. In what had to be her earliest memory, Presley could still conjure up the smell as a horse and rider whizzed past her and her dad at the circus. The riders in that dazzling act seemed to have a telepathic link to their animals that had fascinated her ever since. Presley had always wanted to feel that magic. She knew that if she just had the chance, being around horses would change her life forever. They were perfect animals. Gigantic? Check. Beautiful? Check. Smelly-in-a-good way? Double check. Horses had it all!

But Presley knew that the only way her stepdad would ever agree to let her go would be if she got her mom's permission first. And even though she knew she probably wouldn't be able to do much more than watch, at least that was something. She told everyone that she would be a vet when she grew up, but if she was being honest with herself, what she really wanted to do was be a professional equestrian. Which was maybe going to be a little tough since she hadn't ever *touched* a horse in real life. But Presley was nothing if not determined, even if it meant doing the impossible and changing her mother's mind about horses.

Even though she'd never even been close enough to touch a horse didn't mean she didn't know anything about them. She'd read every nonfiction book about horses in the library. Presley liked to read the science books and the histories more than the novels. She could make up horsey adventures and stories all day long—when Presley read, she wanted facts. She watched the big events like the Kentucky Three-Day Event and the Olympics online, and she'd saved up to collect toy versions of her dream horses. When Presley was interested in something she tried to learn everything she could about it, and she'd been in love with horses her whole life.

Even though she'd forbidden Presley to ride, Mom couldn't possibly be mad if Presley just *went* to a barn. Especially with Mahal. Especially if he *had* to go. It was for work, after all. But Presley knew that she would be in big trouble if she didn't at least *try* to ask for her mom's permission. She also knew that the all-staff meeting at her mom's restaurant started at four thirty and went right up until the doors opened at five and the dinner rush began, and trying to talk to her mom during that time for anything less than the zombie apocalypse was a great way for Presley to get grounded. Instead, she pulled out her phone and composed a carefully worded text to her mom—a text she knew Mom wouldn't see until it was too late.

Mahal walked into his office just as Presley sent off her text.

"Ready to go, kiddo? We've got to get Ahmed from soccer practice and then meet your mom at the restaurant for dinner. Time's a-wasting."

Ahmed was Presley's half brother, born just a year after Mom married Mahal, when Presley was six years old. He was a pest, and also Presley's favorite person in the whole world. He had their mom's tight black curls and wide, easy smile, but his skin was a little closer to Mahal's light brown Egyptian complexion than Mom's dark mahogany. He and Presley shared the same deep brown eyes, goofy sense of humor, and, of course, the family stubbornness.

"We can't!" Presley blurted. She'd forgotten about Ahmed and his soccer practice.

Mahal raised an eyebrow at her, waiting for her to explain.

"Dr. Peters needs your help with a pre-purchase exam at Windy Creek Stables," Presley told him, and scrambled furiously to figure out how to make her plan work. "I bet Gabe and Rishi can pick Ahmed up from soccer, and Mom can bring dinner home from the restaurant instead of us going there."

"You've thought this through, haven't you?" Mahal asked, eyes twinkling as he began to see his stepdaughter's scheme unfold. "And what about you? Are you going to wait here until I'm done?"

"I'll go with you!" Presley said, crossing her fingers for luck. "I won't get in the way, I promise. And I can help."

"Your mom doesn't—"

"I already texted her, so she knows where I'll be," Presley interrupted him even though she knew it was rude. "I'll be with you and Dr. Peters. I won't even get near the horses unless you say it's safe. Mom will be okay, I promise. It's not like I'm going to steal a horse and ride off into the sunset." Then, under her breath, she muttered, "That's not until at least phase six of the plan."

Mahal glanced at his watch. "How about we call her and ask, just in case?"

"She'll be busy," Presley said. "You know how she gets if we interrupt her all-staff meeting."

Her mom's restaurant was a local institution,

serving an eclectic mix of food from the African diaspora and specials that showcased local farms' produce. She'd worked hard to train a staff that was almost like a family. And even though she worked through the opening rush almost every day, she made a point of getting home for dinner with her family every single night. "Pretty please? I'll clean the cat boxes at home *and* here for a month. I'll help Ahmed with his math homework. I'll get up early and take Kierkegaard for an extra walk every day."

"You really want to go to Windy Creek that badly?" Mahal asked. "Pre-purchase exams aren't very exciting and they take a really long time."

"Not exciting to you, maybe," Presley assured him. "But I might get to pet a horse. *In real life.* I really want to go."

"Okay. But I'm going to text your mom too."

Presley grimaced, knowing that her mom wasn't going to be at all happy. But even if she had to suffer through a lecture, she couldn't help but be excited. She didn't just want to pet a horse: She wanted to ride and compete and spend every second of every day around horses. And maybe, just maybe, if she did everything exactly right, this trip to Windy Creek Stables would be the beginning of all of her dreams coming true.

Chapter Two

Presley pressed her face against the truck window as they rumbled down the wide, oak-lined drive that led to Windy Creek Stables. She'd driven past it before, of course. Windy Creek Stables was just off the main road in their little town of Rose Hill, Virginia. It was hard to miss a place like Windy Creek, with its rolling green pastures, white-painted fences, and big green barn. Not to mention the horses. Every time her parents drove past the farm, she wished the clock would slow down so that she could spend more time staring at the horses in the pasture.

As Dr. Peters drove the truck up the gravel driveway, he told Mahal about the horse they were examining. "She's a ten-year-old Andalusian mare that's a prospect for a pair of sisters. They both do a little bit of trick riding, but they're mainly eventers."

"Andalusians aren't usually eventing horses, are they, Dr. Peters?" Presley asked.

"Good catch," Dr. Peters said, smiling at her in the rearview mirror. "Eventing is one of those sports that attracts all kinds of horses, but Andalusians aren't really known for their jumping skills. That said, this little mare took her current owner through training level easily last season."

"Why's she selling?" Mahal asked.

"Tracie said that the current owner is going away to college overseas and can't take the horse with her, but she's determined to see her go to a good home."

"If anyone can find the right fit for a horse, it's Tracie," Mahal agreed.

Presley sighed. If she ever had a horse of her own there's no way she'd choose college over her horse. Some people really had all the luck. As the truck continued down the drive, Presley contemplated whether horses got their own passports when they traveled overseas. Were they fingerprinted, or rather, hoof-printed? These *important* questions consumed Presley's attention until she felt the truck roll to a stop.

Presley bounced out of the truck and took a deep breath of the fresh, grassy air scented with the sweet musty smell of horses. It took her right back to the circus where she'd gotten her magical first glimpse of what horses could do.

"That smell is a time machine!" Presley shouted as she ran around to Mahal's door to open it for him before he could even unbuckle his seat belt.

He shook his head sternly and said, "No yelling around the horses, Presley. Okay?"

But he wasn't doing anything to disguise his wide smile, so she knew he wasn't mad. She nodded solemnly and mimed zipping her lips.

"You know I haven't done a PPE since vet school, right?" Mahal asked Dr. Peters. In their small vet practice, Dr. Peters was in charge of all things equine while Mahal took care of the more exotic animals like snakes and birds, and they shared responsibility for the cats and dogs that came into the clinic.

"Have you even *seen* a horse in this century?" Presley teased.

"You calling me old, kiddo?" Mahal asked, laughing. "I'm not the one with white hair."

Dr. Peters looked in the truck's side mirror and dramatically clapped a hand to his snowy white hair. "When did I get so old?" he gasped, letting his vet bag fall to the gravel. "I'm ancient! Infirm! Presley, fetch me my cane! Mahal, call the retirement home and tell them I'm coming."

Just then, a tall white woman wearing a gray T-shirt emblazoned with the Windy Creek logo tucked into blue breeches, knee socks with carrots on them, and a baseball cap stepped out of the barn. An electric-pink cast was wrapped around her left arm, and a sling held it close to her body. Seeing the spectacle that Dr. Peters was causing, she put her good hand on her hip and failed miserably at looking stern.

"You causing trouble, Dr. Peters?" she asked, striding confidently over to the truck. She hugged Dr. Peters and Mahal before offering Presley her hand to shake. "I'm Tracie."

A little awed, Presley shook her hand. "I know who you are. I watch your dressage test on Felix at last year's Kentucky Three-Day Event on YouTube all the time."

Mahal elbowed her gently. "This is my stepdaughter, Presley. She's usually got better manners than this. As you can see, she's in a bit of a horse girl phase."

Presley glared at him, blushing furiously at having her manners called out but determined to defend herself. "It's not a phase! I've always loved horses."

"Why don't you come take some lessons?" Tracie

asked, winking at Mahal. "We know that being a horse girl isn't a phase around here."

"Mom won't let me," Presley said, trying not to sound sullen. "She's scared of them."

Tracie and Mahal exchanged a knowing grown-up look over Presley's head, and Tracie said, "I see. Well, do you want to come meet Isolde? She's the mare we're doing the PPE on today."

Tracie led them into the barn, and Presley took in everything, gulping down sights and sounds and smells like she'd just found an oasis in the middle of a desert. The barn was U-shaped, with neat rows of stalls on either side joined in the middle by a corridor with wash stalls and crossties on one side and tack rooms, feed rooms, and offices on the other. Horses peeked out over stall doors, soft music played over the speakers, and barn cats tumbled in the aisle. Presley stopped to pet a tuxedo cat named Spur she recognized from the vet clinic. He butted his head into her hand, purring, and Presley thought that Spur was the luckiest cat in the world to get to live at Windy Creek. It was perfect.

Sort of.

Even in the magic of her first time in a barn, Presley noticed that the horse blankets were piled in heaps on top of trunks at the ends of the rather dusty aisles.

Clean and dirty saddle pads were jumbled together against the back wall of the tack room, and a tangle of bridles hung on a hook in the corner, grass clinging to the dull-looking bits. As they passed the feed room, she noticed plastic jugs of supplements scattered across a sticky countertop with stalagmites of sweet feed growing in the corners. For such a beautiful barn, it sure did seem like a lot of chores were going undone.

It was *dirty*. And *disorganized*. Presley must have watched dozens of barn tours on YouTube and none of them had been this . . . Presley wasn't sure what the right word was. It wasn't disgusting—not in the same way the chicken coop got if she didn't clean it for a while. It was just . . . wrong. She'd seen so many pictures and videos of how to take care of tack and make sure your barn was spick and span, and this was not it.

Tracie, having shown Mahal and Dr. Peters where to unpack their things, came over to talk to her. "The barn isn't usually this messy," she confessed. "I haven't quite been able to keep up since I got hurt. All my energy's been going into making sure the animals are taken care of, and not so much into keeping things neat and tidy."

"How'd you hurt your arm?" Presley asked, feeling

guilty for having been so judgmental about the state of the barn.

"I broke it on a cross-country course. My fault," Tracie said. "I got distracted thinking about a mistake I made in the dressage, not the jump right in front of me. My horse went one way and I went the other. Broke my arm in three places and needed surgery to fix it. Also broke a few ribs and punctured a lung. The ribs hurt way worse than the arm, believe me. Luckily, Nightshine wasn't hurt."

Presley's eyes went wide. "*You* fell off your horse? But you're a professional!"

"Even professionals make mistakes," Tracie said with a chuckle. "I forgot the first rule of being around horses. You have to stay in the moment. You can't let yourself think about anything other than you and your horse. Getting distracted is getting hurt. Nearly every time."

"Have you hurt yourself riding before?" Presley asked.

"Of course," Tracie said. "It's a dangerous sport, and it's fair that your mom worries. But it's also a calling. I love riding and I love horses. I can't imagine doing anything else with my life."

"Hear that?" Presley said to Mahal. "It's a calling."

Mahal cut his eyes to Dr. Peters and said, "The only calling I hear is my stomach telling me it's time for dinner. Want to get this show on the road?"

"They're bringing Isolde in from the pasture now," Tracie said. "She's been here on a trial for about two weeks. I like her a lot, and I think the girls do too. Just doing our due diligence before they make an offer. I don't think there's anything to worry about."

As if she'd heard them talking about her, a girl came around the corner leading an enormous white horse. She was the most beautiful creature Presley had ever seen. And the biggest. Presley knew that horses were big animals, but there was a difference between knowing a thing and seeing it. Without thinking, Presley took a step backward and ran into her stepdad.

Presley's heart thumped hard and fast in her chest, like a nervous rabbit. She curled the ends of her bright blue braids tightly around her fist and tugged just a little. Presley realized that she was a tiny bit afraid. She didn't expect that seeing a horse up close would scare her, but it kind of did. It was just so *huge*.

Mahal put a reassuring hand on her shoulder. "You okay?" he asked.

Presley nodded, deciding to make it true. She knew that sometimes things were scary for a reason. Her mom had made that *very* clear. But Presley suspected that sometimes feeling afraid was a little more about how hard the thing felt than it was about real danger. This horse, Isolde, was huge, but that wasn't any reason for Presley to be afraid.

Just as she'd resolved to be brave, another girl appeared beside Isolde. Not just any girl, either. *Harper Lawrence.*

The same Harper who'd been in school with Presley since kindergarten. The same Harper who won every spelling bee, dominated every dodgeball game, and was every teacher's pet. The same Harper who'd never spoken a single word to Presley. Not one. Not ever.

Presley had always thought Harper was kind of stuck up. A Goody Two-shoes with a mean streak, like the girls she always hung out with at school. Not that Presley was a troublemaker; she just didn't really care that much what people thought of her. She wore the clothes she wanted to wear, listened to the music she liked, even if no one else did, and made friends with whoever she wanted—regardless of how popular or cool other people thought they were.

She and Harper didn't have anything in common. Or so Presley thought.

Chapter Three

Presley had always been a schemer, and part of scheming is learning to fly by the seat of your breeches. And even though Harper and Presley had about eight years of the *opposite* of friendship between them, Presley didn't want to let *anything* ruin the precious time she had at the barn. So, Presley decided to treat Harper like she was one of Presley's oldest friends and hope that Harper wouldn't act so stuck up that Presley let the act slip.

"Hey, Harper," Presley said. "I didn't know you were into horses too!"

Harper blinked her big, owlish brown eyes a couple of times and furrowed her eyebrows like she was trying to remember who, exactly, Presley was. "Too?" she asked, echoing Presley. "You ride?"

As the teenager, who Presley assumed was Harper's older sister, led Isolde into the crossties, and Mahal and Dr. Peters got to work, Presley sidled up to Harper. "Not yet," she said. "But I'm going to start taking lessons soon."

It wasn't a lie, she told herself, if she could find a way to make it true. And once Presley decided to do a thing, it got done. She just wasn't quite sure how she'd manage to convince her parents. Yet.

"That's awesome," Harper said enthusiastically, surprising Presley. "Are you going to take lessons here?"

"I want to!" Presley said, studying Harper, whose eyes were trained on the big white horse in the crossties. In all the years they'd gone to school together, Presley had never seen Harper this excited about anything. It seemed to Presley like Harper pretty much only spent time with Amy Mahnken, the most popular girl in their grade, and her tight-knit circle of friends who all dressed the same, talked alike, and had an uncanny ability to make teachers love them.

When they'd been in the third grade Amy had stuck a wad of gum into Presley's hair during science. It had taken several long, painful hours for Presley and her mom to get the sticky mess out so that Presley wouldn't have to cut her natural hair. Presley had held a grudge against Amy and all her friends ever since.

To break the uncomfortable silence that had settled between Presley and Harper, Presley asked, "How long have you been riding?"

"Most of my life," Harper answered, lighting up like a neon sign. "My mom rode growing up, and she put my sister and me in lessons almost as soon as we could walk. It's my favorite thing in the world."

"How did I not know this about you?" Presley blurted.

Harper grinned and bumped Presley with her shoulder. "You've never talked to me before."

"*You've* never talked to *me*!" Presley exclaimed. "You're always with Amy, and Amy *clearly* doesn't like me."

"I'm pretty sure the only person Amy likes is herself," Harper said with an apologetic shrug.

Presley's eyes went wide. "I thought she was your best friend."

"I've known her my whole life. Her dad is a partner in my mama's law firm, and I guess sometimes it's just easier to stay friends with someone who maybe isn't your favorite than to make a fuss." Harper looked over at Presley sheepishly. "You know what I mean?"

Presley definitely did *not* know what Harper meant,

but she was realizing that maybe she didn't know Harper as well as she'd thought she did. "So, who is your best friend if it's not Amy?" Presley asked.

Harper gave her a sly smile. "Does a horse count? Because if so, I have someone I want to introduce you to."

The girls collapsed into each other in a fit of giggles, and Presley was delighted to find that Harper actually seemed nice. Apparently, there was something to the whole "don't judge a book by its cover" thing. Harper might be popular, polished, and pretty, but she wasn't the snobby, stuck-up brat that Presley had always assumed.

"Do you want to show Presley around the barn while we're doing the physical exam?" Tracie asked Harper. "We'll grab you before we do the movement and flexion tests."

"That's the most interesting part," Harper told Presley confidently. "Come on! I'll take you to meet Penelope."

"Who's Penelope?" Presley asked, feeling like she should know the answer.

"My best friend!" Harper said.

"Your horse?" Presley asked. "But I thought you were buying Isolde?" She followed Harper away from the grown-ups and down the barn aisle. Harper must have all the luck, she thought. Not only had she gotten to start riding when she was a tiny little kid, but she had more than one horse of her very own.

"I hope so," Harper said. "I really like her, and she knows *so* much. I feel like I could learn a lot from riding her. But Penelope was my first horse. She'll always be my favorite. Plus, I'll have to share Isolde with Marnie."

"Marnie's your sister, right?" Presley asked.

"Yeah. She's fifteen and has already shown through prelim."

Presley filed the unfamiliar term away to look up later. She was usually willing to admit when she didn't know something, but she wasn't quite ready to let Harper know just how little she really knew about horses. She worried that Harper might think less of her, or worse, use her lack of knowledge against her the way Amy would have. Presley wasn't a naturally suspicious person, but even though she was really starting to like Harper, she still felt a little cautious.

"What kind of horse is Penelope?" Presley asked.

"She's actually a pony," Harper said a little shyly. "She's a Chincoteague pony. You know? Like in *Misty of Chincoteague*?"

Presley had seen the book at the library, but she almost never checked out anything from the fiction section. She tried to remember something—anything—she knew about Chincoteague ponies, but aside from the fact that they were a breed that existed, she had nothing. "I haven't read it," she admitted.

Linking her arm with Presley's, Harper giggled infectiously. "It's the best book!" She paused, considering, and amended her statement. "Other than *The Hero and the Crown*. Or *The Grey Horse*. Or the Saddle Club series, of course. And I know that the Temeraire series isn't about horses, but I kind of like to think that the way the dragons act in those books is how it would be if our horses could actually talk to us."

Catching Harper's enthusiasm, Presley cut in. "It sounds like I have a lot of reading to do!"

"I'll let you borrow all my copies," Harper promised. She stopped in front of a stall halfway down the aisle and went to open the latch but paused. "Have you ever been around a horse in real life before?"

Presley, feeling embarrassed about her lack of experience, shook her head. There was no fudging her way through this one. "I've read a lot, though," she offered. "Books about horse care and horse history and veterinary care and stuff. I like learning."

Harper smiled warmly. "Better than me! I hate reading nonfiction almost as much as I hate studying. Give me a novel any day, but don't make me read about real stuff. Even horses."

That surprised Presley. Harper was always getting awards in school and all the teachers loved her. Presley wondered how she did it if she hated to study.

"Anyway," Harper said. "I'm sure you already know this, but even though Penelope is about a billion years old and has been around kids since the dawn of time, keep an eye on her feet—getting stepped on really hurts—and if you need to walk behind her, stay really close and put a hand on her butt or stay far away so you don't get kicked."

"And if I feed her anything, do it with my hand flat?" Presley offered.

"You're a natural!" Harper said, pulling a peppermint out of her pocket and handing it to Presley. "Give Penelope one of those and you'll be her favorite person in the world."

Presley followed Harper into the stall where a fat brown pony stood munching on a pile of hay. She looked up at the girls when they opened the door and went right back to her snack, utterly disinterested. Even though she was just a pony, Presley was surprised by how much space she took up. Penelope was nearly as tall as Presley, and Harper, who was a couple of inches shorter, could just barely see over her pony's back. More impressive, though, was the fact that Penelope was as round and fat as a barrel. Her glossy brown coat stretched over her big tummy, and her thick, bushy mane and tail stuck out in every direction.

"She's huge," Presley exclaimed. "Are you sure she's a pony?"

Harper laughed and gave the pony a gentle scratch behind her cheekbone. "She sure is. The bravest, best pony I've ever known. She's worth every coin of twelve silver pennies!"

"Twelve silver pennies?" Presley asked, curiously.

"It's from *The Lord of the Rings*," Harper said with a sheepish smile. "Bill the Pony is one of my favorite characters in those books. Penelope reminds me a little of Bill."

Presley realized that Harper was just as much a nerd as she was—just about different things. Presley may have read every nonfiction book in the library about horses, horsemanship, and the evolution of her favorite animal, but Harper had spent just as much time reading about horses. She just had the benefit of getting to learn about horses in real life, so she'd read fiction instead.

Breaking Presley out of her reverie, Harper asked, "Do you want to give her the peppermint?"

Presley unwrapped the candy and held it out to the pony on the flat of her palm. Penelope snorted and whirled around to face her, snatched the peppermint out of Presley's hand, and pushed her big, heavy nose into Presley's hips, throwing her off balance. Presley stumbled backward in a panic, tripped over her own feet, and fell against the stall door with a loud clang.

The big brown pony whinnied and stamped her feet, flashing her steel-shod hooves. Presley scrambled backward out of the stall and away from the startled pony. Her heart battered the insides of her ribs, making it hard to catch her breath. Presley *knew* how dangerous horses—even small ones—could be, and the last thing she wanted was to get hurt. If she managed to injure herself just giving a horse a treat, there was no way her mom would ever let her ride.

"Get out of there, Harper!" Presley warned. She didn't want her new friend to get hurt.

But Harper wasn't scared at all. Instead, she'd moved closer to Penelope's head and was patting her calmingly and whispering to her. As if by magic, the pony transformed from the enormous, ferocious warhorse that Presley had been terrified by back into the fat little pony just looking for an extra treat or two.

"What a bad pony," Harper scolded lovingly as she scratched Penelope's neck. "I'm sorry she scared you, Presley. I should have warned you that she can be a little bit pushy when it comes to peppermints. Do you want to try again?"

Determined not to let something as silly as a little fear get between her and her dreams, Presley plastered a smile on her face and strode back into the stall. "What should I do differently?" she asked.

"Nothing," Harper said. "It wasn't your fault at all. Just remember that you're the boss, and if she tries to push you around, you push right back. She's not allowed to beg, and she knows it. She just saw a new face as an easy target."

With Harper's encouragement, this time felt different. Penelope snuffled her velvet-soft lips over Presley's hand and delicately retrieved her treat. Even as she was crunching the peppermint in her mouth she started sniffing at Presley's hips, giving her gentle little nudges.

Presley gave her a gentle nudge back, but Penelope ignored her, snuffling at Presley's pockets. "Now what?" she asked Harper helplessly. The question of what to do about a persistent and pushy pony hadn't been covered in any of the books that Presley had read.

Harper shoved Penelope's head away from Presley with an indulgent little chuckle. "I've always been taught that you ask a horse to do what you want nicely once, firmly a second time, and if they still don't listen, you have to tell them in a way that makes them sit up and pay attention. It works with most horses, but Penelope's spoiled and rude."

Presley agreed with Harper, but she wasn't about to say that. She'd be devastated if one of her new friends didn't like Kierkegaard or Bisous or one of her other pets. And it wasn't that she didn't like Penelope. She really did.

"Can I give her some scratches?" Presley asked.

"Sure! She loves getting the spot right under her cheekbones scratched. Like this," Harper said, showing Presley what to do.

Presley imitated Harper, scratching the pony's cheekbone first gently, then harder, as Penelope pushed into her hand.

"You found her spot," Harper said, smiling. "You're a natural."

"I don't know about all that," Presley said, still petting the pony. "I've wanted to ride all my life. But my mom's terrified that I'll get hurt. I don't know if seeing the instructor in a cast is the best way to change her mind."

"Parents," Harper said knowingly, "sometimes have to be shown what's best for their kids."

Presley tried to put on an expression that showed Harper that she totally knew what she meant, but the thought of Penelope's quick movement, flashing hooves, and enormous strength stuck to her like a cocklebur made of doubt. What if her mom had been right all along? What if horses really *were* too dangerous?

Harper waved a hand in front of Presley's face, bringing her back to reality. "You checked all the way out. Where'd you go just now?"

Presley shrugged like it was no big deal and went back to petting the pony's soft neck.

Harper, addressing Penelope, who'd started nosing around her pockets, said, "That's all for now, P. Gotta earn your treats."

Penelope huffed out a breath and turned, heading toward the window. Extremely aware of the pony's hooves, Presley took a quick step back. A quick, *squishy* step back. Groaning, she looked down. Her white Converse sneaker was ankle deep in a pile of pony poop.

"Oh no!" Harper said, looking around the stall like there might be a switch to flip to take back the last thirty seconds. "I'm so sorry. I was supposed to clean P's stall before we got Isolde in, but Mom was running late. Let's go see if we can find you a pair of shoes to borrow. Ones that are less enpoopled."

"Enpoopled?!"

"Yeah," Harper said. "Like ensorcelled. But, you know, with poop."

Presley chuckled. "At least it doesn't smell as bad as llama poop," she said.

Harper quirked a quizzical brow at her. "Llama poop?"

"My stepdad's a vet," Presley explained. "I'm an expert in all things animal poop. Ask me anything."

Harper snorted as she closed Penelope's stall behind her. "You're pretty cool, Presley Elder."

"You're not so bad yourself, Harper Lawrence."

Glowing with the promise of a new friendship, Presley followed Harper back down the barn aisle toward the tack room, taking in the warm, musty smell of the horses and their hay, the last light of the spring evening filtering through the dust motes, and the peaceful sound of the horses munching on their dinners. It would have been an absolutely perfect moment—something out of a movie—if it weren't for the chaos at the edges.

Chapter Four

The tack room was overrun with the kind of mess that drove Presley up a wall. Tangles of halters lay haphazardly on top of tack trunks. Blankets were piled into corners, collecting dust. Everywhere she looked, Presley discovered a new kingdom of horrors to haunt the fussy perfectionist that lived in her bones. Saddle pads were slumped in heaps against the walls, clumps of red clay clung to grooming buckets and trailed across the floor, and leather straps spilled out of tack trunks around the room.

"Is it always this . . ." Presley searched for a polite way to say what she was thinking.

"Messy?" Harper finished for her.

Presley caught her lip between her teeth, cringing. She didn't want to imply that the beautiful stable was anything less than perfect. But the whole place felt kind of neglected. "I was going to say disorganized," Presley offered, not even trying to sell the lie.

"It's a mess," Harper confirmed. "All of us are trying to lend a hand, but Tracie's assistant trainer took most of the horses to Florida to train for the winter, and her barn manager quit right before her accident."

"She can't hire someone else?" Presley asked.

"She's only in the cast for another few weeks. I guess she thought she could handle it until she found the right person." Harper shrugged, digging into a trunk overflowing with helmets, boots, and other bits of riding gear. "What size shoes do you wear?"

Presley told her, nervously fiddling with a knotted ball of leather straps that she *thought* might be a bridle.

Harper fished a pair of bright purple cowboy boots from the depths of the trunk and offered them to Presley. "These are a half size too big, but they should work. You can bring them back the next time you're here."

The next time I'm here, Presley thought. *What if this is the last chance I get?* She needed to find a way to come back. To make herself useful. To make the lie she'd told Harper about starting to take lessons true. She'd gotten a taste of the horse world, and she couldn't imagine going back.

"Do you want to have a sleepover this weekend?" Harper asked, breaking Presley's sad train of thought. "You could come to the barn with me after school on Friday and then stay the night."

"I want to!" Presley said excitedly, but then remembered her mom's rules. "But I'll have to ask."

"And convince your mom?" Harper asked.

Presley nodded forlornly. "I don't even know if that's possible."

"Put those boots on," Harper commanded. "And I'll show you how it's done."

Presley did as she was told, gingerly slipping her enpoopled sneakers off and shoving her feet into the boots. "Do you even wear boots like this for English riding?" she asked.

"Absolutely not," Harper said, laughing. "Those have probably been here since Tracie was a little kid."

Presley looked down at her newly shod feet. "I kind of like them. These puppies could have walked out of the Hyer Brothers boot store back in 1875!"

I don't think Tracie is *that* old," Harper said, looking at Presley quizzically. "The who brothers?

"Oh! The modern cowboy boot design is said to have come from these two brothers in Kansas in the late 1800s!" Presley told her enthusiastically.

"How do you know this stuff?" Harper asked.

"How did you remember that Bill the Pony cost twelve silver pennies?" Presley countered.

"Fair enough," Harper said, looking her up and down, from her electric-blue box braids to her faded vintage band T-shirt and then on to her black jeans shoved into the antique purple boots. "It's a look," she said. "That's for sure."

Presley did a little spin. "I'm an equestrian fashion icon," she told Harper confidently.

"Girls," a woman's voice called. "Harper? Presley? It's time! You want to come to the arena and watch?"

Harper's eyes lit up like a pair of blue ribbons. "Let's go," she said, and took off out of the tack room at a power walk. Presley jogged to catch up, but before they got to the indoor arena Harper put out a hand to slow her down. "No running around the horses," she told Presley. "Might spook them."

Presley nodded, blushing that she didn't realize something so obvious and filing the rule away in her mind so that she didn't forget it. "Sorry!"

"It's okay!" Harper said. "You didn't know!"

"I'm going to figure this all out, you know," Presley told her.

"I know!"

"I am!"

"I believe you," Harper assured her with a laugh. "Sheesh! I'd hate to get between you and something you really want to do. Your mom's about to have a fight on her hands."

In the arena, two unfamiliar women were standing around the big white mare with Mahal, Dr. Peters, and Tracie. One was nearly as tall as Mahal, with the same rich, shiny brown hair and pale complexion that Harper had. The other woman was much shorter and rounder, with warm, maple-brown skin. She wore her silver-gray curls cropped close to her head, and when she heard the girls, she turned her wide, bright smile on them.

Harper speed walked over to the women and wrapped her arms around them both. "Mama!" she said, greeting the shorter woman. "I didn't know you were coming."

"I had to see if we were getting ourselves a fancy new pony or not, didn't I?"

The other woman turned to look at Presley. "Who's this, then?"

Smiling, Harper introduced Presley to her parents. "Mom, Mama, this is my friend Presley. She's going to start taking lessons here soon," Harper said, giving

Presley a knowing look. "Can she spend the night on Friday?"

Presley cut her eyes to her stepdad to gauge his reaction. The smile creeping across his face told her that his narrowed eyes and furrowed brows were all an act. Mahal secretly loved watching Presley scheme and connive to get her way. After all, Presley told herself, her schemes usually meant that he ended up with a lot fewer chores to do, even if the other consequence was that her mom was nearly always exasperated by the two of them.

"May I?" Presley asked, being sure to say "may" instead of "can" because her stepdad was a real stickler for good grammar.

"Only if your mom says yes," he cautioned.

Isolde stamped one long, white leg impatiently, and Dr. Peters patted her forehead fondly. "I know, girl," he mock-whispered at her. "We just have to be patient while the girls try to pull the wool over all these grown-ups' eyes."

"And what are you, if not a grown-up?" Tracie asked playfully.

"An objective third-party observer," Dr. Peters said with a wink at Presley and Harper. "An advocate for the independence of young people. A man whose dinner is getting cold while we wait around to figure out what exactly these two are scheming over."

Harper's moms led the girls over to the viewing deck in the indoor arena to watch the rest of the examination. Dr. Peters flexed Isolde's legs and had Mahal trot her around, explaining each test he was doing, what he saw, and what the test told him about Isolde. Finally, he looked at Tracie and said, "I know Isolde has been on trial, but if the girls want to get on her, I'm happy to assess her under saddle as well."

"Girls? Which of you wants to do the honors?" one of Harper's moms asked.

Harper pursed her lips and glanced at where Marnie was sitting a few seats over on the observation deck, eyes trained on her phone. She waited a second before prompting her older sister. "Marnie? Do you want to ride?"

Marnie, without looking up, said, "Nah. I've ridden her three times this week already. You go ahead."

"She's texting her boyfriend," Harper said to Presley conspiratorially. "Will you feel totally left out if I go ride for a few minutes?"

Presley, surprised that Harper would even ask, shook her head. "Of course not! I can't wait to see you ride!"

Grinning, Harper took off at the fastest walk Presley had ever seen and appeared down in the arena just a few minutes later, balancing a bunch of tack. She moved like a whirlwind around Isolde, who was calmly accepting affectionate pats from Tracie, Dr. Peters, and Mahal. Soon, Isolde was fully tacked up in a shiny black leather saddle and bridle, sparkly lavender saddle pad, and matching sparkly lavender bonnet and boots. Harper buckled her helmet on, and, with the help of a leg up from Tracie, was sitting on Isolde, as easy as can be.

Presley looked on in awe as Harper transformed from just another kid into *an equestrian*. That was the only way that Presley could explain it. Harper guided Isolde around the arena, the big white mare arching her neck and letting her long tail flow out behind her like a flag. Tracie asked Harper to pick up a trot, and almost immediately Isolde's gait changed. Presley could have sworn that Harper didn't move her body at all. She rode with her back straight and her hands out in front of her, moving with Isolde. It was like watching an illustration of the perfect rider come to life. Presley didn't know if she was impressed or intimidated or both.

But when Tracie told Harper to canter, Presley's jaw nearly dropped wide open. She didn't just *want* to learn to ride like Harper, she *needed* to. The way the horse and the girl moved together was like magic—and not something out of one of Harper's novels—this was real, actual magic. Presley could have watched Harper ride forever, but eventually Tracie called for her to cool Isolde off and untack her. The grown-ups all clustered together to talk about grown-up stuff and Presley followed Marnie down to the crossties where Harper was untacking Isolde.

"Do you think that you're going to buy her?" Presley asked Harper and Marnie.

"Unless Dr. Peters found something wild in the X-rays, probably," Marnie answered.

Harper punched her sister in the arm. "Don't say that! It's bad luck!"

Marnie brushed Harper away like she was nothing more than a horsefly, and without looking up from her phone, said, "But he probably wouldn't have suggested we ride if he did. Good job, by the way. Those canter transitions were nice."

Harper turned back to Isolde, but not before Presley caught the look of pride on her face. Harper really looked up to her older sister. In just a couple of hours Presley had learned more about Harper than she had in all the years they'd been in school together.

By the time Dr. Peters and Mahal had packed up their supplies and finished talking to the other adults, the girls had exchanged phone numbers, followed each other on social media, and agreed to meet up at lunch the next day to plan their sleepover. Presley was pleasantly surprised by just how wrong she'd been about Harper and how much she was looking forward to getting to know her better.

Chapter Five

Presley couldn't get a word in edgewise that night at the dinner table. Between Gabe and Rishi quizzing each other to prepare for their history test, Ahmed's endless stream of anime plotlines and facts, and the bits of boring adult talk that Mom and Mahal snuck in at every (infrequent) lull in the conversation, Presley didn't stand a chance. Not unless she wanted Mom to scold her for interrupting. And the last thing Presley needed right now was for her mom to be even slightly annoyed with her.

As soon as she'd cleaned her plate—even the brussels sprouts—Presley politely asked, "May I be excused? I'm finished."

That was enough to bring the conversation to a screeching halt. Presley was never the first to leave the table—mainly because she refused to finish her vegetables most of the time. In fact, she had secretly waged a long con with her mother by pretending to despise several types of vegetables that her mom and Mahal cooked all the time—brussels sprouts, okra, beets, that kind of thing. Presley actually liked brussels sprouts and okra, but she also liked the bonus points she got from her mom by strategically eating them without complaint from time to time.

"What'd you do?" Gabe asked.

"Did you fail a test or something?" Rishi piled on.

Gleeful, Ahmed joined in. "Presley's in trouble!"

"Am not!" Presley exclaimed, letting her annoyance get the better of her. Then, seeing the wary look on Mom's face, she got nervous. "I was just hungry."

Presley's mom glanced at her empty plate, suspiciously eying the place where the brussels sprouts had been, and narrowed her eyes. *Her long con was a secret, right?* she worried.

"Presley made a friend at Windy Creek Stables today," Mahal offered. "She wants to go to a sleepover on Friday."

"Windy Creek *Stables*," Mom repeated, serving Presley and Mahal her most devastating glare and pulling her phone out of her pocket. "Ah yes," she said to Presley dramatically. "Here's the text message you sent. 'Mahal's gotta do a house call for work. Rishi and Gabe are gonna pick up Ahmed. Love you.'"

Mahal cleared his throat, but Presley came to his defense before he could say anything. "Dr. Peters needed Mahal's help with a pre-purchase exam. He texted you too, right?"

"This isn't about your stepfather, young lady," Mom said. "What is our rule about horses?"

Years of lectures about all the dangers of horses hung in the empty space around Mom's words. But she didn't repeat herself. She didn't raise her voice. All she did—and it was more than enough—was wait. Eventually, between the weight of her mother's silence and the excited, slightly terrified looks on her siblings' faces, Presley cracked.

"I didn't break any rules, Mom! Promise."

Presley cut her eyes to her siblings. All three of them had abandoned their dinner in favor of the show that always came around when Presley and Mom tested their wills against each other. Most of the time, Mom won and Presley ended up with half of their chores. This time, Presley was determined to come out on top.

"Aren't you always saying that I need another

after-school activity, like a sport or something, for college?" Presley asked her mom with a sweet smile.

"Horseback riding isn't a sport," Mom said.

Presley was outraged. "It's in the Olympics. It's *totally* a sport. And maybe I'll hate it. Why don't you just let me take a lesson or two and see? Remember how long I begged you for oboe lessons?"

Gabe and Rishi exchanged a look and immediately collapsed into giggles. Presley couldn't blame them. Her oboe playing had lasted for exactly one practice session, which had ended up with their dog, Kierkegaard, playing dead in the living room.

"Tracie's a good teacher," Mahal offered. "She's smart and sensible and runs a nice little barn."

"She's a *professional*," Presley said. "One of the horses she trained went to the Olympics."

"Didn't she break her wrist just recently?" Mom asked. "She was wearing a cast when she came into the restaurant last week."

"She did," Mahal said.

At the same time Presley corrected her, "It was her arm." Presley didn't add that Tracie had also broken a few ribs and punctured her lung. She knew that wouldn't help, and moreover, she wasn't going to change her Mom's mind about horses. Not that night anyway.

"Wrist? Arm?" Mom said. "Both prove my point. Horses are dangerous. I like Tracie. She's a good customer and seems like a good person, but that doesn't mean that's going to change my mind about my daughter being around big, dangerous animals. That's final."

Instead of pressing the issue, Presley changed tactics. "Anyway, Harper asked me if I could spend the night on Friday. May I? Please?"

"I'll have to talk to her parents," Mom said automatically. "Have her mom or dad call me. And you have to finish your homework and your chores. Before you go. Tonight. No excuses."

"Moms," Presley corrected. "She has two moms. I'll do all my homework *and* extra credit!"

Mom sighed and rubbed the bridge of her nose. "The child could be the ward of a dragon or a long-lost princess being looked after by a coven of witches. I'd still want to talk to whatever adult was the boss of them before I let you stay over at their house, okay?"

"She'd like that," Presley said. "She's really into fantasy novels."

Presley washed the dishes after dinner, helped feed all the animals, and even offered to help Ahmed with his reading homework before Mom shooed her off to start getting ready for bed.

Presley's room was on the very top floor of their old, rambling Victorian house, in what had once been the attic. The walls sloped inward, creating four little nooks in the room. One for reading, one for sleeping, one for playing, and one for work. Over the years she'd covered the walls in pictures of her favorite professional riders torn from magazines, posters of the bands she loved, and quotes from her favorite riders. Her parents had even let her paint and draw on the drywall, connecting her decorations with scenes of horses galloping across open fields, faeries playing in the fence lines behind famous cross-country jumps, and little nods to interesting bits of equine evolution and history. It got a little warm in the summertime, but she'd sweat all day if it meant not having to share a room with Rishi and her never-ending phone calls about whatever it was that high schoolers spent all their time thinking about. Prom? Algebra homework? Lacrosse practice? Presley just didn't want to listen to it.

After she brushed her teeth, washed her face, and got into her pajamas and bonnet, Presley pulled out her phone to text Harper.

My mom wants to talk to yours before she says yes to a sleepover. 😊 *But! First! Did you buy Isolde?*

The text bubble that showed Harper was typing appeared immediately, and Presley hoped that Harper wouldn't think she was a total loser because of her mom's rules.

YES! Harper sent the text with an effect that filled the whole screen with the word. Her next text appeared just a second later, chasing the last like a dog going after a ball.

I was just about to text you the same thing. Send me your mom's #. My moms are SO strict.

Presley sent her mom's contact to Harper, relieved to know that she wasn't the only kid that had to live with a ton of rules. She typed, *I thought having an older sibling was supposed to make them LESS strict, not more. I swear mine are way easier on the older kids than they are with me.*

Presley had a theory about older siblings. Rishi and Gabe were boring. They didn't care that Mom and Mahal were strict because they didn't *want* to do anything interesting. They were happy to play their sports, do their homework, and practice their instruments. Presley had never been like that. She wanted to gallop through life, devouring everything she encountered. Presley had an endless appetite for knowledge and risk. That day she'd gotten one step closer to the thing she wanted to do more than anything else in the world: ride horses. And she might have even found herself a friend along the way.

Chapter Six

"What are the rules?" Mom asked for the millionth time as they pulled into the school parking lot on Friday morning.

Presley forced herself to keep a straight face and answer politely. She couldn't risk Mom changing her mind at the last minute, and even a tiny hint of attitude from Presley would see her spending her weekend scrubbing pots at the restaurant instead of hanging out with Harper at Windy Creek.

"Be polite," Presley recited. "Say please and thank you. Offer to help."

"And?" Mom prompted.

"No riding," Presley said, exasperation creeping into her voice.

"Not even for a second," Mom confirmed. "You should be glad that I'm even letting you go watch Harper's lesson."

"I am," Presley agreed. "So glad. Very grateful. You're the best mother in the whole entire world."

In the back seat Ahmed whined. "I'm gonna be late!"

"Sorry, A!" Presley said as she scooped up her backpack and overnight bag and slid out of the car. *Freedom at last,* she thought. But before she made it to the school's door, the worst thing imaginable happened. Her mom rolled down the car's window and yelled, "Remember to call me to say good night! I love you!"

Wilting from embarrassment, Presley forced something that could have been mistaken for a smile onto her face and turned to wave goodbye. Luckily, it was already hot and there weren't too many other kids outside witnessing her humiliation. It was like her mom didn't realize she was almost twelve. Ugh.

Presley sailed through her classes on a cloud of excitement and anticipation. She was going to a *barn* for the second time in a week. She was going to pet a horse. And, while she was there, she was going to figure out a way to convince her mom to let her ride.

As soon as the last bell rang, Presley raced to her locker, grabbed her overnight bag, and found Harper waiting for her at the front of the school. They walked across the street to the high school to meet Marnie and Harper's mom.

"I'm so excited that you're going to be there for my first lesson with Isolde as *my* horse," Harper said to Presley.

"Our horse, comrade," Marnie corrected, not looking up from her phone.

Harper gave Presley an exasperated look that Presley immediately recognized. Older siblings were the worst.

"Want to help me get her groomed and tacked up?" Harper asked, checking her watch for the third time in as many minutes.

"She'll be here soon," Marnie scolded. "Stop checking your watch. You're not going to be late for your lesson."

Presley, who had a lot of experience with annoyed elder siblings, did her best to break the tension with a question. "Will you teach me? I've read about it, of course, but I've never done it."

"Definitely!" Harper said. "We're going to have so much fun!"

"Sweet!" Presley said with a sly smile. "I wouldn't want to do it wrong and make Isolde look *tacky*."

Harper and Marnie's groans echoed around Presley in a surround-sound chorus of dismay as Harper's mom pulled up in her fancy white SUV and Marnie hopped into the front seat. Harper and Presley piled into the back and found a couple of bottles of water and baggies of trail mix waiting for them in the center console. On the way to the barn Harper's mom peppered them with questions about their classes, their teachers, and how much homework they had to do over the weekend. Marnie, eyes locked on her phone screen, gave surly, one-word answers, while Presley did her best to show off the good manners her own parents had enforced every day of her life. But the whole time she was practically vibrating with anticipation.

The second the car stopped in front of the big green barn, Harper and Presley jumped out. Arm in arm, they power walked inside. It took all of Presley's self-control to keep from running down the aisle and petting every perfect velvety nose along the way. The huge animals weren't quite as intimidating up close when it was just their heads reaching out over their stall doors to say hello. She waited, rather impatiently, while Harper got changed into her breeches, and then it was finally time to get to the good stuff—the horses.

Presley followed Harper out to the paddock where Isolde was happily munching grass with a small group of other horses. "Why are some of the horses in stalls and others aren't?" she asked.

"Some of the horses get turned out for part of the day or overnight, depending on the weather, and others live outside all the time. It kind of depends on what the owner can afford and what the horses like best. Some horses hate being inside, but all horses need time outside to graze and relax and just be horses."

Presley yodeled enthusiastically, "Jeeeeealooooous!"

Harper snorted and asked, "About what?"

"Horses just being horses," Presley explained. "If you can be anything, be a horse. If you can't be a horse, then be yourself."

Harper laughed. "Who're you quoting?"

Presley considered. "Myself? Circa . . . just now?"

Harper groaned.

"You like my jokes," Presley told her confidently.

Harper cut her eyes at Presley and nodded. Presley could tell that she was trying hard to look very, very serious.

Presley eyed the red clay mud along the fence line and changed the subject. "What if they get dirty?"

"They're animals," Harper said, laughing. "They'll

always get dirty. Especially grays like Isolde. Gray horses love rolling in mud."

"I thought Isolde was white?"

"There really aren't white horses," Harper told her. "Horses like Isolde with all-white coats are usually born brown or black or even dark gray."

"What color was Isolde when she was a foal?" Presley asked, proud that she didn't even have to search her mind for the word for baby horses. All baby horses were called foals, but the boys were colts and the girls were fillies. Everything in the horse world had its own special name. Even though Presley had read and watched a ton of stuff about horses, there were so many things that she didn't know or couldn't remember.

"Isolde was born a bay—brown with a black mane and tail. Tracie knows the person who imported her, and she gave us baby pictures. Most Andalusians like Isolde go gray, but some of them stay bay or black," Harper said, pulling her phone out of her pocket and scrolling through her photos before she pulled up one of a scruffy brown foal with gangly legs and showed Presley. "They look a little mangy when they're little and shedding out their first coats."

Presley looked from the goofy little brown baby on

Harper's phone to the majestic white horse grazing calmly in the pasture. "I don't usually say this, but that baby is way cuter as a grown-up."

Harper took a bright pink halter and lead rope from a hook on the fence and looped the rope over her shoulder. She unhooked a chain and held the gate open for Presley. The horses looked up as they walked into the paddock but quickly went back to their grazing.

"How do you get her to come to you?" Presley asked. "Do you whistle?"

"Like for a dog?" Harper asked.

Presley's face got hot from embarrassment, and she wondered why she'd asked such a silly question. Horses and dogs were totally different. "Sorry," she muttered. "That was a bad question."

"There's no such thing," Harper assured her. "And some horses do come when you whistle or cluck or call their name. I mean, Shadowfax came when Gandalf whistled, right? I just don't really know Isolde that well. We only had her on trial for two weeks."

Feeling a little braver with Harper's reassurance, Presley asked, "So how do you catch her?"

Harper touched the halter hanging over her shoulder and explained, "Most horses, you just kinda go up to them and put the halter on. Some are a little harder to catch and you have to train them, but Tracie's lesson horses are pretty good about it. Isolde is funny about having her face touched, so you have to be really quiet and gentle with her. Want to watch this time and next time you can try?"

Presley agreed and hung back watching as her new friend made her way over to the white—

No. She corrected herself. *Gray. Isolde is a gray mare.*

Harper approached Isolde's shoulder, speaking softly. She looped the lead rope around Isolde's neck and waited patiently for the mare to put her head up. When Isolde finally lifted her head, Harper slipped the halter on and fastened it before giving Isolde a hearty scratch on her neck.

As they walked Isolde out of the pasture and back to the barn, Harper told Presley that even though she and Marnie were technically sharing Isolde, Marnie was leasing one of Tracie's upper-level eventing horses while Tracie recovered from her injuries. That meant that the big gray horse was basically Harper's for now, anyway.

"Marnie helps keep Tracie's horse in shape *and* she can get experience riding and showing an upper-level horse. It's a win for everyone," Harper told Presley.

That sparked something in Presley's mind, and she

struggled to dig up the right word from everything she'd read. "Is Marnie Tracie's . . . intern?"

Harper looked confused, but after a second, she said, "Do you mean working student?"

"That's the word I was looking for!" Presley confirmed.

"Tracie doesn't have a working student right now," Harper said. "Her last one left right after Tracie got hurt. Pearl wanted to be with someone who was actually competing this season."

Presley made a face.

"Tracie says that she did what she thought she had to do," Harper said with a shrug as she led Isolde into one of the wash racks. She hooked the long leads to either side of Isolde's halter, undid the lead rope, and hung it on a hook before turning to Presley with a sly smile. "Pearl was super stuck up, and I'm glad she's gone. She didn't deserve to learn from a trainer as accomplished as Tracie if she couldn't stick around to see if Tracie was going to be able to compete again."

That confused Presley. "I thought she just broke some bones. Why would that keep her from competing again someday?"

Harper paused in front of a shelf full of grooming buckets and turned around to look at Presley.

"Tracie didn't *just* break *some* bones. She almost died. I thought you knew. I thought that was why your mom didn't want you to ride."

Presley felt a pit open up in her stomach. She'd always known—and been constantly reminded by her mother—how dangerous riding was, but actually knowing someone who'd had a bad accident made her mom's fears feel a lot more real.

Chapter Seven

Even though Harper went out of her way to explain everything step-by-step while she tacked Isolde up for her lesson, Presley was distracted. She felt like the flag tied to the middle of a tug-of-war rope. On one side, the fear of horses her mother had tried to explain to Presley her whole life had suddenly grown arms and started pulling—hard—against Presley's determination to make her own dreams of galloping over jumps and bringing home blue ribbons come true. Before Harper took Isolde into the indoor arena, she reminded Presley where the observation deck was so that she could sit and watch the lesson.

Presley stepped through the lounge where heavy, well-loved leather couches formed a horseshoe around a coffee table and TV. Ribbons seemed to grow from the wall behind the TV like flowers—blue and red and yellow ribbons of all sizes were pinned over one another without any rhyme or reason. It was beautiful. The other walls were covered in photos of smiling people on horseback. Ancient black-and-white photographs of people wearing old-timey riding clothes and top hats were mixed in among newer photos. Presley studied the people in the photos, chewing on the inside of her cheek as she realized the part her mom hadn't ever said out loud. Every single person in the photos was white.

Presley knew that horses, riding, and Black people had a complicated history—just like everything in America was complicated by race and history—but the way her mom told it, the danger and expense of the sport had always been the thing that stood between Presley and horses.

Just then, Presley heard a voice come booming over the loudspeaker. "Isolde's had a few days off, so let's take our time in the warmup. Let's start out with a nice, relaxed walk. Remember to push her forward into the contact with your legs and seat; don't pull her toward you with the reins."

Not wanting to miss anything, Presley slipped through the big glass doors and took a seat on the deck next to Harper's mom. The indoor ring was huge, with jumps set up on one side and an ankle-height white fence marked with letters enclosing the other. Marnie was mounted on an enormous brown horse whose lavender saddle pad matched his leg wraps—polo wraps, Presley reminded herself—and Marnie's shirt. He swished around the arena like he was floating with his neck arched prettily. Even though Marnie didn't seem to be doing anything at all up there, Presley knew she was probably working really hard.

Harper, on the other hand, was struggling.

"Harper, stop pulling on her face," Tracie instructed. "Do you see how she puts her head way up in the air every time you tug on the reins? She's trying to get away from the contact instead of reaching for it."

Harper grimaced and adjusted her hands, but Isolde kept reaching forward with her head and tugging the reins away from Harper.

"Marnie, how about you work on getting Felix bending and flexing, okay?" Tracie said. "Start with spiraling in and back out of a twenty-meter circle at the trot, then take him down the quarter line and leg yield him out to the wall. Both sides. Harper, bring Isolde over here."

As far away from Harper and Isolde as she was up on the observation deck, Presley could see the bright red blush racing up Harper's neck and across her face. She knew how frustrating it was to have someone else watching you try to do something you'd done a thousand times before. Somehow, having an audience made everything way harder. Presley thought Harper was brave for *letting* Presley come watch her lesson. She really hoped her new friend wasn't regretting it now.

Presley recognized some of the terms Tracie was using, like "trot"—the gait between walking and cantering—and "leg yield"—one of the odd dance-like movements in dressage that was almost like side stepping and walking forward at the same time. But the more she hung around Harper, the more she realized how little she knew. Like, how on earth could someone just *know* what twenty meters even looked like?

Tracie disappeared for a second, and when she reappeared she was carrying a long white rope. It looked like the lead rope that Harper had used to bring Isolde in from the pasture, but way, way longer. She looped the end with the clip through the metal ring on one side of Isolde's bit, over her head, and clipped it to the other side of the bit.

Then she did something that made Presley sit up and pay attention. She took the reins off of Isolde's bridle. Presley looked over at Harper's mom, but she was paying a lot more attention to the computer open on her lap than she was to her girls' riding lessons.

Isolde flicked her ears and shifted her weight, but continued to stand peacefully in place as Tracie took a few steps back, still holding onto the rope.

"Every once in a while," Tracie said to Harper, "it's a good idea to go back to basics. I think you're worrying a lot more about the way Isolde *looks* than how she *feels*. Did your last instructor ever talk about the Dressage Pyramid of Training?"

That, Presley recognized. It was something that she'd memorized in one of her horse books because it seemed so important. As Harper recited the six concepts, Presley muttered them under her breath as well.

"Rhythm. Relaxation. Connection. Impulsion. Straightness. Collection."

"Good job," Tracie praised Harper. "Does that give you a hint about what's going on with Isolde right now?"

Harper pressed her lips together so tightly her mouth nearly disappeared and shook her head no. Presley *hated* it when grown-ups asked her questions that they already knew the answers to. She wondered if Harper did too.

"You're worrying about collection before you even start thinking about anything else. You're working from the top down instead of going from the bottom up. That's why it feels like you're riding a baby octopus instead of a horse. Isolde doesn't know what you're asking her to do," Tracie said.

Even before Tracie finished talking, Harper's expression cleared and she started to nod.

"What I want you to do is stop worrying about Isolde's head, stop worrying about collecting her. I just want you to focus on controlling her rhythm with your seat and legs. Bring her up to a walk."

For the next half hour Tracie held the lunge line while Harper rode Isolde, and Presley watched, amazed, as her friend and her friend's horse relaxed and started working together. By the time Tracie reattached the reins to Isolde's bridle and let the horse off the lunge line, Harper was able to get the white—gray—mare to walk, trot, and canter and then go back to walking all just by using her legs and what Tracie kept calling her "seat."

The second half of the lesson, Tracie turned her attention to Marnie—walking her through how to move her body *just so* to get Felix to do a complicated dressage move—while Harper practiced what she'd just learned. Presley was transfixed. She finally understood why, hundreds and hundreds of years ago, Grecians might have mistaken people on horseback for centaurs. When Marnie rode, it was nearly impossible to tell what the horse was choosing to do and what Marnie was asking for. It was like they were one mind sharing two bodies. Presley may have thought she'd been hooked before, but after watching the way that a person and a horse could form a partnership and move together, Presley knew that she didn't just *want* to ride horses.

She *needed* to learn to ride. And she'd find a way to make that happen. No matter what.

Chapter Eight

Even though it was just her second time in the barn, Presley already felt more comfortable around Isolde and the other horses. Harper showed her how to take off Isolde's saddle, trade her bridle for her halter, and hook her into the crossties. As Harper hosed cold water over Isolde's legs, she wiped the sweat dripping from her red face. Presley looked around for her friend's water bottle, but didn't see it with Harper's grooming kit.

"Do you want me to take over for a minute so you can cool off?" Presley offered.

"It's the rules. My moms and Tracie say we've gotta take care of our horses before we take care of ourselves," Harper said with a wry smile. "It was one of the reasons that Mom wanted to move to Tracie's barn in the first place. Tracie wouldn't like it if I asked you to do my work for me."

"I get that taking care of your horse is kinda like a chore, but would they really care if you took a tiny break to get some water?" Presley asked.

"Isolde comes first," Harper explained. "Grooms took care of almost everything at our last barn. They taught us how to do stuff, but they didn't expect us to ever tack up or do any other chores. Mom wanted me and Marnie to be responsible for our horses."

"That makes sense," Presley agreed, thinking about her own animals at home. "I bet you learn a lot from how they act when you're grooming and tacking up and stuff."

"Yep!" Harper agreed as she turned the hose off and searched through her grooming kit for something. She stood up holding a piece of pink plastic, kind of like a long butter knife. "Same way you learn from doing all kinds of barn chores. Feeding, cleaning stalls—all of it makes you a better equestrian."

"Sign me up," Presley said, holding out her hand for the tool Harper was holding. "Teach me your horse girl ways, please."

"You sure?" Harper asked, looking hopeful. And sweaty. Very sweaty. "It's probably okay for me to get my water as long as Isolde is being taken care of."

Presley nodded eagerly.

Harper handed it over and started to head toward the lounge. She paused halfway across the barn aisle and turned around with a sheepish grin. "Do you know what that is?"

"It looks like a butter knife, but I'm pretty sure Isolde doesn't need to get covered in peanut butter or jelly," Presley joked, and both girls giggled hard.

"You're like my working student," Harper teased in a singsong voice as she came over and showed Presley how to drag the plastic tool—it was called a sweat scraper—across Isolde's coat to pull the water off her and help her cool down.

"You're a natural!" Harper complimented between big gulps of water when she reappeared a moment later with her pink, aluminum bottle.

As she helped Harper finish taking care of Isolde and turn her back out in the pasture with her friends, Presley was making mental notes.

1. Shavings and spiderwebs growing up and reaching down corners of the barn like stalagmites and stalactites.
2. Blankets gathering dust in haphazard piles.
3. Tangles of baling twine ready to be eaten by barn cats—Presley had spent enough time in

a vet's office to know how dangerous string really was for curious cats, and she had a special place in her heart for the Windy Creek barn cats, Spur and Ariat.
4. Sticky counters growing mountain ranges of supplement dust like topographical maps in the feed room.
5. Pieces of long-neglected tack turning strange colors in the corners of the tack rooms.

The chaos in the barn was making Presley think. Tracie needed help. And Presley was just the person to volunteer. While Harper and Marnie were changing back into their street clothes and their mom was taking a phone call outside the barn, Presley gathered her courage and knocked on the barn's office door.

"Come in," Tracie's voice answered.

Presley pushed the door open and waited for Tracie to look up from her computer. Unlike in the lounge, the photos framed on the walls of the office all featured one girl. She shared Tracie's wide smile, her freckles, and her thick, curly hair. In some of the photos, a man with kind, hooded eyes and straight black hair held hands with Tracie or the little girl who shared some of his East Asian features.

"Is that your little girl?" Presley asked after a few moments had passed in silence.

Tracie looked up at Presley with a warm smile. "Natalie," she said. "She's twelve. About the same as you?"

Presley nodded. "I bet she's a great rider."

Tracie shook her head. "She's allergic, unfortunately. But she does come visit. I'm sure you'll meet her if you hang around."

"That's what I wanted to talk to you about," Presley said. "My mom is really scared of me learning to ride. But I wondered if maybe I could help you out after school and on the weekends. Even if she won't let me ride, I really want to be around horses."

Tracie studied her, letting the silence between them grow until Presley felt like she could feel it crawling up her legs like a million little bugs. She *had* to say something.

"I noticed there were some chores and cleaning that needed to be done. And it's not like, you know, child labor or anything," Presley added quickly. "I'd be volunteering. So that I could learn. Like a working student."

"She's read every horse book ever," Harper's voice came from over her shoulder, and she threaded her arm through Presley's, stepping into the doorway beside her. "And she can come with me after school. Mom won't mind giving her a ride."

Tracie raised one eyebrow. Presley wondered if that look was like car seats: Parents weren't *allowed* to leave the hospital until they knew how to make kids squirm with a look.

"I'll work hard, and I won't be in your way. I promise," Presley said.

"Why don't you write down your mom's phone number, and I'll give her a call tonight to talk through it," Tracie said, finally letting a smile creep onto her face.

"Really?" Presley asked, excitement foaming out of her like bubbles overflowing from a shaken Sprite.

"No promises," Tracie said, holding up her hands. "But I do need the help, and your mom, Mahal, and I have known each other for a long time. I'll see what I can do."

"You're a real sucker for a horse girl, Tracie," Harper's mom said cheerfully as she poked her head into the office and put one hand on each girl's shoulder. "Let me get these rascals out of your hair. We'll see you soon."

"Bye, Tracie," Harper said, as her mom steered them toward the car.

"Thank you," Presley called over her shoulder.

On the car ride back to Harper's house, Harper talked about everything she'd learned in her lesson and everything she wanted to practice over the next week. Even though Presley was interested in what her new friend had to say, a part of her was nervous about how the conversation between Tracie and her mom would go. She thought that she should call her mom and warn her that the horse trainer would be calling. But that part was really tiny compared to how much she was hoping that Tracie might be able to convince Presley's mom to give her a chance at the barn—if she didn't have enough time to put together an argument against it.

Chapter Nine

The next morning, Presley stretched herself awake beneath the canopy of Harper's spare bed. A spare bed with a canopy all its own wasn't the only difference between Harper's house and Presley's. Harper was *rich*. That had always been clear—her clothes were always fashionable and new, she got dropped off at school in nice cars, and she had two horses of her very own (mostly). But Presley hadn't really understood how wealthy her friend was. Not until Harper's mom pulled up to the big, wrought iron gate that stretched across their driveway.

Harper wasn't just "my mama's a lawyer and my mom owns a business" rich. No. Harper was reality-TV rich. Mansion rich. Live-in-staff rich. No wonder she could afford to have multiple horses. But, Presley acknowledged, it really didn't seem to go to Harper's head. She might have seemed stuck up in school, but since they'd found their shared love of horses, Presley had come to see that Harper wasn't really a snob. She was just shy.

"You want to see if there's anything to eat?" Harper asked, yawning.

Presley checked her phone. No texts or calls from her mom. She wondered if Tracie had forgotten to call. "My mom's supposed to pick me up at ten," she said. "I should probably get my stuff together before she gets here."

"It's only nine thirty," Harper said. "And I'm so hungry. I bet Marta got the good pastries from the farmer's market. Meet you in the kitchen when you're done packing?"

"If I can find my way," Presley said. "This place is a maze."

Harper threw a pillow across the room, but her aim was terrible and Presley barely had to duck to avoid it. "It's too much house," she agreed. "But I'll wait for you. Don't want you to meet one of Marnie's pet cheetahs alone in the hallway."

Presley looked up, eyes wide, not sure if she was excited or terrified. Harper grabbed a ball of yarn from a canvas tote hanging on the back of her closet door and began to unravel it as she backed out of the room.

"Don't worry," Harper said, unable to contain her giggles. "I'll leave you a clew so you can find your way through the maaaaze."

Bewildered, Presley asked, "A clue, like, to a mystery? I don't get it."

Harper stopped, put her hands on her hips, and said, "No, a clew! It's what balls of yarn or cord used to be called. The princess Ariadne used a clew to help Theseus escape the Minotaur and the Labyrinth."

Yawning, Presley said, "Well, how about that. Learn something every day around you. Wait, I thought you mostly read fantasy about horses?"

Harper's voice came echoing from a distance down the hall as she continued to lay out yarn. "What do you think pulled everyone's chariots, numb nut!"

The girls had just piled their plates with freshly grilled challah French toast, berries, and maple syrup when the doorbell rang. The kind-faced Swedish housekeeper, Marta, wiped her hands on her apron, but before she could turn the stove off, Harper had hopped up and taken off running for the front door.

"I got it," she hollered over her shoulder.

A moment later, she reappeared, leading Presley's mom by the hand. "Mrs. Elder-Sharaf, I would like you to meet Ms. Marta Magnusson," she said with an exaggerated bow. "Marta is the only reason that us Lawrence kids have made it past our toddler years and into our childhoods."

"I'm sure your parents would be just thrilled to hear you say that," Marta admonished.

Just then, the patio door opened, and Harper's moms walked in. "It's the truth," Harper's mama said, holding out her hand for Presley's mom to shake. "I'm Marjorie, and this is my wife Augustine. We've both been huge fans of your restaurant since it opened."

Presley watched her mom shake hands with Harper's moms, searching her for a sign that she'd spoken to Tracie, but she kept her face impassive and calm—her restaurant mask, as Gabe called it. "Thank you so much," Presley's mom said. "I hope Presley wasn't any trouble."

"Not at all," Marjorie said. "August picked them up from school yesterday and took them to the barn. Apparently, Presley was a huge help to Harper and even offered to help Tracie while she recovers from her last injury. You've got a good kid on your hands."

"I heard something about that. We'll have to see," Presley's mom said.

"She was great," Harper piped up. "Presley's got the touch."

Presley shot Harper a discouraging look. Her mom hated being pressed. Especially in front of other parents. She thought that Harper would have understood that. But every family was different, and Harper's moms clearly operated differently than Presley's parents. Lights-out was strictly enforced at Harper's house, but bedtime had long since faded from the priority list at Presley's mom's house and her dad's. However, Presley couldn't remember the last supper that didn't include a salad, and dinner at Harper's the night before had been a smorgasbord of takeout because, as Harper had explained, Thursdays and Fridays were Marta's days off and Harper's moms didn't cook.

"Why don't you go grab your stuff, Pres?" Presley's mom said, ignoring Harper's comment. "We're going to have to get moving if we want to make it to Ahmed's game."

That was when Presley knew she was in trouble. She gave her mom the required, "Yes, ma'am," and slinked out of the vast kitchen. She and Harper exchanged promises to call each other later that night to study for their social studies test, and as Presley closed the old Volvo's door, she felt the weight of her mom's irritation settle over her like a wet blanket.

"You should have talked to me *before* you tried to get your scheme started," Mom said, her voice strung tight with disappointment.

"I *have*," Presley reminded her. "I've wanted to learn to ride for years. You know that."

Mom drove on in silence for a few minutes, avoiding Presley's eyes in the rearview mirror. Eventually, Presley looked out the window instead. It was a lost cause. Her mom was never going to understand. She was never going to agree. Presley was going to have to wait until she was a grown-up to get to learn to do this one thing—the thing she wanted most in the world. She felt hot tears pricking at the corners of her eyes, but she swallowed hard and pushed the sadness down into her belly. Crying wouldn't do her any good. Not right now at least. When she was home, and in her attic surrounded by her pets, then she would have a nice, long cry before she figured out her next plan. Presley was a lot of things, but she wasn't the kind of person to give up on her dreams.

When they pulled into a parking spot at the soccer complex, Presley fumbled with her seat belt latch, trying to get out of the car before her mom saw the tears that had the audacity to escape Presley's resolve and slide down her cheeks.

"Pres," Mom said, flicking the child lock to keep her from opening the door. "Wait a second."

Presley paused, her hand on the door, waiting for Mom to say whatever it was she felt like she had to get out. Presley hated disappointing her parents. But it was even worse when they were disappointing her right back.

"You know that your grandparents never wanted me to open the restaurant, right?" Mom asked.

Presley nodded. The story was vaguely familiar. "They wanted you to be a doctor."

"They saw that I loved taking care of people," Mom said. "But I would have made a terrible doctor."

"That's why you don't like going to the clinic with Mahal," Presley said, not sure where her mom was going with the story. "It makes you sad."

"Yes," Mom said. "But that's not the reason I didn't want to be a doctor. I loved cooking more than anything else in the world. I spent all my time thinking up recipes and testing them out. But my parents wanted me to be safe. They felt like the life of a chef was unpredictable, and they wanted a more stable, predictable life for me. Your dad reminded me of that last night."

"You talked to dad?" Presley asked. "Why?"

Mom chuckled. "We may be divorced, but we're both still your parents, Presley. After Tracie called me, I called your dad. He asked me if I would have been happy working in medicine. And the truth is, cooking for a living may be risky, but it makes me happy. I want you to be happy too, Presley."

Presley glanced up at Mom, trying to get a hint of what she was trying to say from the look on her face.

"Last night Tracie said to me that some people are just born horse people. That it's a calling, and I could stop you from answering it now and hope you grow out of it. But I want you to know *why* I've never wanted you to ride. Are you okay with me telling you a hard story?"

Presley nodded, but she felt sick to her stomach, knowing that this was her mom's way of letting her down easy. Presley, after all, liked having all the facts, and her mom knew that better than almost anyone.

"When I was a kid, my best friend was a girl named Heidi. I'm sure you've heard me talk about her."

Presley nodded. Heidi's dad had served with Grandpa in the military, and they'd been stationed together all over the world. Mom-and-Heidi adventure stories were Ahmed's favorites, just like Presley had loved them when she was his age. Heidi had died before Presley was born, but Presley felt like she knew her all the same.

"Well, I've never told you one really important thing about Heidi. She was just as horse crazy as you are," Mom said, lacing her fingers together and squeezing her hands between her knees anxiously.

That made Presley sit up straight. "Really? What—"

Before she could ask any of the thousand questions galloping through her mind, Mom interrupted her.

"When we were seventeen, Heidi was competing at a huge hunter jumper show in Delaware, and by then Dad was stationed at Annapolis, so I drove over to watch her ride." Mom took a shaky breath and reached out to squeeze Presley's hand. "Honey, Heidi died that day. She and her horse fell over one of the jumps and she broke her neck. She was a great rider. Fearless, like you. And dedicated. She cared about those horses more than anything else in the world. You would have loved her."

The slime-slick feeling of fear and regret for disappointing her mom yet again surged back up Presley's throat, and she swallowed hard, trying to keep the tears at bay.

"I get it," Presley said. She'd spent years scanning

the internet for statistics that made horseback riding look less scary or dangerous but hadn't found anything that she thought might convince her mom. The data didn't lie.

But even if Presley had found the data to back up her argument, her mom's story would have popped that balloon anyway. Horseback riding *was* dangerous. Her mom had lost her best friend to a horseback riding accident. But even that didn't make Presley want to do it any less.

Resigned, Presley said, "I didn't mean to scare—"

"But," Mom interrupted, "if Heidi knew I was keeping my own daughter away from horses when she *clearly* has the calling, she'd never let me hear the end of it. I respect that this is something you want to try. Something that you might love. And I could help you learn how to do it from the best. Safely. So, here's the deal."

Impressed by Presley's audacity and enthusiasm, Tracie had offered to let Presley volunteer to help around the barn. In exchange for cleaning stalls and doing barn chores after school three days a week, Tracie would give Presley a lesson every week *and* a practice ride. Presley's mom only wanted one thing in exchange: a promise that Presley will be extra, super careful, follow all the rules, and do her very, very best to never fall off.

Giddy with excitement, Presley pulled her cell phone out of her pocket and pretended to answer a call, "Yeah, who is this? Gravity? Never heard of you, lose my number! I'm not falling. Off anything. Ever again." She looked over at her mom and said, "Click"—through what had to be the biggest grin in the observable universe.

Chapter Ten

Presley couldn't wait to tell Harper the news, and as soon as she sat down in the stands with her family, she texted her. She spent all of Ahmed's soccer game with her nose buried in her phone, planning out every last detail of her first day of volunteering at the barn with her new friend. Much to her chagrin, she had to wait three full days—Sunday, Monday, and Tuesday—before it was time to go back to the best place in the whole world. The barn.

With Harper's help, Presley planned her perfect first-day outfit from the bottom up. She wore the cowboy boots she'd borrowed from the barn, an old pair of jeans, and, even though Harper had told her to wear things that she didn't care that much about, Presley couldn't help choosing her favorite T-shirt, a vintage Paramore tour shirt that had been her mom's. She wanted to make a good impression on all the horses, after all. And what better way to do that than by showing off her great taste in music?

Marta picked the girls up from school and took them across town to Windy Creek. Tracie was waiting for them in the office with a cheery smile and a to-do list as long as her arm.

"I know you won't get to all of this today, or even this week," Tracie said. "But there are always things to do around the barn, and the more you do, the more you learn!"

"Can I use the outdoor arena to work with Isolde after I get Presley started?" Harper asked.

Tracie's eyebrows shot up, and her face broke into a slow, wicked smile as she looked Harper up and down. "I guess your moms didn't tell you," she said.

"Tell me what?" Harper asked, looking a little afraid.

"They loved Presley's work ethic, and they asked if you might be able to work off the cost of some of your lessons too. You and Presley have the very great honor of being in the first ever class of Windy Creek's Junior Working Student Volunteer Program."

"Don't you have to actually *volunteer* yourself for volunteer work?" Harper grumbled.

"Minors don't," Tracie said cheerfully.

"I knew this would happen," Harper groaned, eyeing the list. "When am I ever going to have time to ride?"

"That's the beauty of Presley's idea," Tracie said. "You get to spend more time at the barn instead of just showing up to ride. If you finish your work quickly, you can ride every time you're here, if you want. And if it's one of Isolde's days off, I'll let you use one of the lesson horses."

That made Harper's eyes light up. "I can choose?"

Tracie studied Harper thoughtfully. "Within reason. And you have to ask first, okay?"

Harper nodded, a slow smile creeping across her face.

"First up, we need to get Presley some equipment. Take a look and see if anything in the sharing bin in the lounge will work for her," Tracie said, eyeing Presley's outfit. "She'll need boots—English paddock boots, not those cowboy boots—breeches, and a helmet. Do you usually wear your hair in box braids?"

"Sometimes," Presley said, wrapping a blue braid around her finger. "Sometimes I put it in twists or bantu knots, and sometimes I just wear it loose."

"Right," Tracie said with a warm smile. "So, it's not really fair, but you may need one helmet for when your hair is in box braids or another style that adds extra volume, and one for when your hair is natural. Helmets are made to sit really snug to your head to keep your skull safe, and the one that works today may not work as well when your hair is in a different style. I can put your parents in touch with some of my Black friends in the industry to get some advice, but in the meantime, let's find something that fits for now."

Presley nodded, a little surprised that Tracie was aware enough to think of that kind of thing. "Thank you," she said. "And after that? What can we do to help *you*?"

"You can scoop some poop," Tracie said with a laugh. "There are always stalls to clean and buckets to scrub around here. Once that's done, you and Harper can check the list."

There were a plethora of used pieces of equipment and riding clothes spilling out of three tack trunks in the lounge. Presley desperately wanted to sort and tidy them, but Harper was itching to get their work done so that she could ride Isolde. It didn't take long for her to load up an empty feed bag with several pairs of breeches, a helmet, and tall boots for Presley.

"You won't need it for a while, but I'm pretty sure that we have a safety vest that will fit you at home," Harper told Presley confidently. "For when you start learning to jump."

"How soon do you think that will be?" Presley asked, leaping over a pile of feed bags on an imaginary steed.

"Don't tell me that Tracie's adopted another stray. The last thing we need around here is one more green rider who has no idea what they're doing and is always asking for help."

Presley and Harper looked up to see Amy—the girl Presley had always assumed was Harper's best friend—leaning against the doorjamb, tapping a crop against her shiny-black tall boots.

"Butt out, Amy," Harper snapped.

That surprised Presley. She'd never heard Harper be so harsh.

"What did I ever do to you?" Amy asked sourly.

"Nothing," Harper said, giving Presley a look that told her it would be better not to ask—not right now at least. "We're about to muck stalls. Want to help?"

"Ew," Amy said. "Isn't that what the hired help is

for? You may want to tie your star to Tracie's latest charity case, but if I'm going to qualify for regionals, I need to practice."

"I guess we've all got different priorities," Harper said. "Come on, Presley. I'll show you where we keep the wheelbarrows."

Harper picked up the feed bag full of Presley's new-to-her gear and brushed past Amy. Suddenly, Presley felt totally out of place in the barn. Between these two white girls with their neat tan breeches and their horse experience, Presley was the fish out of water. She might have had some book knowledge about horses, but that didn't mean she knew how to do anything. They'd both been around horses for years. They had all the right clothes, and both of them knew how to muck stalls and tack up and *ride*.

Presley had chosen the right shirt all right. Her bright-red band T-shirt was just as out of place as she was. She hadn't felt like a charity case. Not until Amy had shown up and treated her like one.

Chapter Eleven

Dejected, Presley followed Harper to one end of the barn aisle, grabbed a pitchfork and a wheelbarrow of her own, and waited for Harper to tell her what to do next. She might be out of place and too far behind to ever catch up to the other girls, but the least she could do was finish what she'd started. Harper stopped her wheelbarrow in front of the first stall and took a good look at Presley.

"Don't let Amy hurt your feelings," Harper said. "She's a bully. When my moms decided to move our horses here and start training with Tracie, I thought that I wouldn't have to see her as much. But of course, Mama told Amy's dad that we were moving barns and now she's here too. I can't escape her."

"Well, now you've got me here, and she *really* doesn't like me," Presley joked. "So maybe she'll leave you alone."

"I doubt it," Harper said darkly, but before Presley could ask what she meant, Harper headed into the stall and looked over her shoulder expectantly, waiting for Presley to follow her.

It didn't take long for Presley to catch on. Mucking stalls was kind of like cleaning cat litter boxes, but on a much, much larger scale. Luckily, horse poop didn't smell nearly as bad as cat—or worse, ferret—poop. Harper and Presley soon developed a system. One of them would pile all the dirty shavings into a wheelbarrow while the other dumped, scrubbed, and refilled the stall's water buckets. Then, while the one who'd cleaned the buckets wheeled the dirty shavings outside and dumped them in the muck pile, the other would start on the buckets in the next stall.

Working together, the girls cleaned all fourteen stalls on the right side of the barn in just over an hour. When they were done, Harper led Presley to the lounge and grabbed a soda for each of them out of the communal fridge. They sprawled onto the cozy leather sofas and silently sipped from their cans while the air-conditioning helped dry their sweat.

"How many more do we have to go?" Presley asked wearily.

"According to Tracie's list," Harper said, looking at the picture she'd taken with her phone, "we can leave the other stalls since those are the horses that get turned out at night, and she doesn't want us cleaning stalls with horses in them. Next thing we've got to do today is clean some bridles and stuff. But if we get through all the tack on Tracie's list, we can do what we want until my mom comes to pick us up."

"What do you want to do?" Presley asked. "Do you want to ride?"

"Sure," Harper said. "But I'd rather wait until Amy's left. Plus, I'm here to help you learn! What do you want to do?"

Presley absently went to chew on her thumbnail—a habit of hers when she was thinking—but stopped herself, remembering just how much poop she'd touched in the last hour. "What's the deal with you and Amy?" she asked instead.

"We used to be best friends," Harper said, and suddenly, Presley saw the same snobby, quiet girl she'd always avoided at school. It was like watching her friend put on a mask, and Presley wasn't sure how to make it go away, but she knew she didn't like it. Not one bit.

Harper continued, "Now we aren't. There's not much more to tell. You ready to get started on the tack?"

"Sure," Presley said. But she was determined to get to the bottom of whatever it was that made Harper close up like that.

The girls gathered a tangled nest of leather and buckles from the corner of the tack room along with a bucket, a tin of saddle soap, sponges, and rags, and plopped into a pair of chairs in the barn aisle to sort through everything. Presley was surprised to find that all of her studying had paid off as she helped Harper sort through the bits of leather and metal, laying them out and matching them up as they worked to untangle the knot of tack.

Harper held up a loop of leather that had a long strap attached to it and studied the dry, stiff leather. "I think this is a running martingale?" she told Presley, sounding a little unsure of herself.

Presley took the piece of tack from her friend and chewed on the inside of her lip, debating with herself about whether or not to correct Harper. It turned out that, after years of studying books about horses, she could easily tell the difference between a running martingale and a standing martingale, and she knew exactly what they were used for.

Deciding that she'd rather know if she got something wrong in the barn than make a mistake a second time, she said, "Isn't it a standing martingale?"

Harper shrugged. "I'm not sure! Penelope goes in a simple bridle and saddle, and we bought Isolde's saddle with her, but aside from a bridle, I don't really know what other tack she needs yet. What's the difference between the two?"

Presley pulled another tangled piece of equipment from the pile—another loop of leather, but instead of just one strap attached to it, this one's attachment split into a Y. Holding it up, she showed Harper the difference.

"See?" she asked. "A running martingale's straps attach to the reins and put pressure on the bit so that the rider has a little bit more leverage, and so that the horse doesn't throw its head up in the air to avoid the bit or hit the person in the face. Standing martingales have straps that attach to the noseband, and they're considered a little more dangerous because the rider can't give the horse more space if it needs it."

"You weren't kidding when you said you'd read a lot about horse stuff," Harper said, gaping at Presley. She grabbed two of the bridles they'd just untangled from the knot of tack and held them up to Presley. "Tell me more stuff! Why are these two bridles so different?"

Laughing, Presley showed off what she knew and made notes in her mind to look up the stuff she didn't. She liked that there were some horse things she knew more about than Harper. It made her feel a little more like she really belonged at Windy Creek.

When they'd put like with like, Harper showed Presley how to rub soap into the leather with a damp sponge and remove all the caked-on grime and sweat and spit before conditioning the leather and hanging it up to dry. The soap smelled good. Not like the harsh chemicals they used to sterilize the vet clinic and the restaurant or the soft floral soaps they used at home. This soap was rich and warm and almost creamy, like lotion. Presley loved it.

But even more, she loved sitting in the barn aisle with Harper, watching people and their horses come and go. There was a little girl she recognized from Ahmed's soccer team, who confidently led and tacked up a leopard-spotted Appaloosa pony. Presley curiously watched a redheaded boy she'd never seen before lead a thick-boned chestnut mare into the crossties across from them. The horse's coat was wavy, like it had been brushed all out of place, but its mane and tail were curly—not as curly as Presley's hair, but curlier than she'd ever seen on a horse.

Presley leaned over to Harper and whispered, "Is that a Bashkir Curly?"

"Good eye!" Marnie said, stepping out of the tack room and surprising Presley so much she nearly jumped out of her skin. "Have you met Frank yet? He's about your age, and he just started last year, but he's a natural."

The boy, Frank, gave Presley and Harper a reluctant smile. "Hey," he said shyly. "Winnie's only half Bashkir. Her mom's a quarter horse and her dad's a Bashkir. But we love her anyway. Do you want to give her a cookie?"

Presley practically jumped out her chair, remembering only at the last second to grab the bridle she'd been working on so it wouldn't fall into the dust and ruin all of her hard work. She accepted the sticky brown ball Frank offered her and looked at him quizzically.

"What kind of cookie is this?" she asked, sniffing it.

Marnie chuckled, and Frank glanced over at Harper, doing his best to keep from smiling. "A German Horse cookie. Want to try it?"

"Don't," Marnie warned.

At the same time, Harper said, "Do it!"

Presley, who was physically incapable of turning down a dare, gave the thing a nibble and made a face. It was kind of sweetish, but that was the only thing the cookie had going for it.

"What's this made out of?" she asked, holding it out to Winnie, who took the cookie delicately from Presley's palm with her soft, velvety lips.

"Just oats, alfalfa, and molasses pretty much," Frank said, studying the back of the bag of treats. "Tracie sometimes makes a people version and a horse version for barn parties. Hers are pretty good."

Presley rubbed Winnie's forehead appreciatively as the horse nuzzled her pockets, looking for more treats. "Who's a good girl?" Presley murmured to the horse. She was getting used to them, she realized. Winnie—which, she had to admit, was a hilarious name for a horse—was way bigger than Penelope, and Presley wasn't scared at all.

"You're a natural," Harper said, still giggling.

Marnie rolled her eyes, pulled her phone out of her pocket, and walked toward the side of the barn where Tracie kept Felix, the big bay Dutch warmblood that Marnie was leasing while Tracie was recovering. Presley, having noticed that Harper said,

"You're a natural!" kind of a lot, smiled to herself. Her siblings got just as annoyed by her own little quirks as Harper's did.

When everything was clean and put away neatly in the tack room, Presley looked around and made a face at Harper. "Why does everything else look worse now that we've gotten some of it clean?"

"Please tell me you don't want to clean the whole tack room today," Harper pleaded. "We can do more next time. Come on. We only have, like, an hour and a half before Mom comes to get us."

An hour and a half seemed like a long time to Presley, but she didn't want to disappoint her new friend, and if she was being honest, she'd rather get some hands-on time with a horse than keep cleaning up after them.

"Do you want to go get Isolde?" Presley asked.

"Yes!" Harper agreed enthusiastically. "You can practice tacking up. You only got to see it twice, and it's a lot to learn."

When Harper swung the pasture gate open, Isolde and the other four mares in the field looked up briefly. One mare, a chestnut with a delicate face and well-muscled body, whinnied loudly. Startled, the bay next to her kicked up a cloud of red dirt with her back feet and took off galloping across the field. A second later, all three of the other horses wheeled and ran off, chasing her. Harper moaned.

"This field is like twenty acres. It'll take fifteen minutes to walk over to them," she complained.

"Why'd they do that?" Presley asked, fascinated.

Harper shrugged, already power walking up the hill toward the cluster of once-again-calm mares. "Dunno. Something spooked Mercy, or, more likely, she thought that we were coming to get her and make her work. She's, like, twenty-five and kind of herd sour."

Seeing Presley's puzzled expression, Harper clarified, "She's really attached to her herd, which makes her misbehave when you ask her to leave them."

"Like separation anxiety in dogs," Presley said. "My stepdad has a Great Dane patient who ate half of his people's front door when they left for work one day."

Harper paused and looked at Presley, horrified. "Was the dog okay?"

"I think so," Presley said. "I mean, he's still a patient. Kind of makes termites seem boring by comparison. Not sure what the people did about their door, though. What do you do for separation anxiety in horses—I mean, horses that are herd sour?"

"I don't really know," Harper said. "We can ask

Tracie or Marnie, though! Marnie's more of a horse fact nerd than you are."

It seemed like Harper really looked up to her sister, and even though Marnie acted just as disinterested in Harper as Gabe and Rishi were in Presley, she liked that Harper didn't hide her admiration to try and act cool. Presley also really liked that Harper was so comfortable admitting that she didn't know something. It wasn't an attitude that came naturally to Presley, but she wanted to adopt it. She was a newbie, after all. Presley wanted to learn everything there was to know about horses, and every time she came to the barn it became more and more clear that she could read all the books in the world, but a million pages wouldn't come close to real life experience.

Chapter Twelve

By the time Presley and Harper caught Isolde, walked her back across the enormous field, and tacked her up, Harper only had about forty-five minutes before her mom got to the barn to pick them up. That sounded like an eternity to Presley, but Harper told her that it was nothing at all in what she called "barn time."

"Barn time?" Presley asked, following Harper down the ramp to the indoor arena.

Harper plucked a long dressage whip from the collection hanging on the wall and said, "Tracie says that scientists should study the phenomenon. Time somehow speeds up at the barn. You think that three hours will be plenty of time to get everything done, but then you do two things and all of a sudden it's been over an hour."

"It's like the opposite of what happens when I'm

diagramming sentences in English class," Presley mused. "I feel like the bell should ring at any second, and then I look up at the clock and it's been, like, three minutes."

Harper giggled and nodded as she led Isolde over to the red plastic mounting block in the corner, checked to makes sure her girth—the belt-like thing that kept the saddle in place—was tight, and put one foot in the stirrup before stopping. "I forgot to tell Tracie I was getting on. It's one of the rules—anyone under eighteen has to make sure that an adult knows they're on a horse, no exceptions. Would you mind letting Tracie know for me?"

Presley nodded. It was a good rule, she thought as she made her way through the barn, looking for Tracie. She found the trainer crouched next to a stocky black-and-white pinto horse with a Roman nose and kind eyes in the crossties, examining a hoof the size of a dinner plate. Presley told her that Harper was riding Isolde in the indoor arena.

"She's wearing her helmet?" Tracie asked, even though it came out more like a command than a question.

"Yes, ma'am," she said, recalling Harper buckling the helmet purposefully under her chin before she unclipped Isolde's pink halter from the crossties and switched it out for her supple, black leather bridle.

"Great. You come get me if she needs anything, okay?"

Presley agreed, but before she could turn around, Tracie asked her to wait. "Can you hand me that Betadine?" she asked. "It's the white plastic bottle behind my right hip."

Puzzled, Presley picked up the bottle—she'd spent enough time at the vet clinic to know that Betadine was used to clean wounds—and placed it in Tracie's good hand. She wanted to know what the horse had done to its hoof and how Tracie was treating it.

"Hard to twist with broken ribs," Tracie explained, answering a question that hadn't even occurred to Presley. She'd been more focused on the horse than why Tracie would need to be handed a bottle that was right next to her. The reminder about Tracie's injury reopened the pit in Presley's stomach, so instead of peppering her with questions, Presley hustled back to the indoor arena to make sure that Harper was all right. She didn't want to leave her friend all alone on her horse.

When Presley reached the top of the ramp that led down to the arena, she paused, hearing raised voices.

"You're going to hurt him."

Harper's voice was sharper than Presley had ever heard it. Presley crept down the ramp, not wanting to get into the middle of a sibling squabble if Harper was arguing with her sister. Coming from a family with three siblings—Presley didn't see any reason to differentiate between her brother, half brother, and stepsister—Presley was well-versed in sibling rivalry.

Pressed flat against the wall next to the crops and dressage whips, Presley peered into the arena. To her surprise, it wasn't Marnie Harper was arguing with. It was Amy. She sat atop a tall, shiny brown horse whose coat was nearly black from sweating.

"He's fine," Amy said. "We barely did anything. Anyway, I'm in a hurry. Mom's picking me up for dinner any minute, and I still need to rinse off and change. I'll give you ten dollars if you'll untack him for me."

Amy's horse looked like he'd done a whole lot more than nothing. Flecks of foamy white sweat gathered on his neck and heaving sides. He looked exhausted. Amy swung one leg over his side and dismounted, tossing his reins over his head and holding them out to Harper.

"Come on," she wheedled. "It's just this once."

"Fine," Harper snapped. "But if Tracie asks why, I'm not covering for you."

"Whatever. We pay her to take care of our horses. Worst case scenario, she's mad at you for taking money out of her pocket," Amy said airily.

In a moment of panic, Presley realized that Amy was going to pass her on her way out of the arena, and she *really* didn't want to look like she'd been eavesdropping. Even though, she admitted to herself, that's exactly what she'd been doing. Presley bent down, pretending to pick something up, just as Amy turned the corner.

"You're still here," she sneered. "Just because Harper is being nice to you now doesn't mean that you're going to fit in here. Windy Creek is a stable for *serious* riders. Not kids who just want to pack around on lesson ponies. You're starting way too late to ever amount to anything. You may as well give up."

"It's not gymnastics or ballet or something that changes the way you grow," Presley retorted. "There are tons of people who started way older than we are and went on to compete at the highest levels. Look at Ian Stark. Or Steph Croxford."

"They were *naturally talented*," Amy said snottily. "That's like a one in a million chance. Plus, they had the time and money to buy excellent horses and pay the best trainers. You're never going to the Olympics on a used-up old lesson horse, and it sure doesn't look like your family has the money to buy you a horse of your own."

That stung. Not because it was true—Presley's mom made sure that all her kids knew *exactly* how privileged they were to live the comfortable life they had. But even though they'd been in school together since kindergarten, Amy hadn't bothered to learn one single thing about Presley. Instead, she was making snap judgments based on nothing more than the way she looked and the way she dressed.

"Clearly, money can't buy talent," Presley muttered icily under her breath, but loud enough that she was sure Amy had heard her.

Amy rolled her eyes and kept walking. Irritated, Presley headed back into the arena. Harper was leading both horses around by their bridles, concern puckering her mouth like she'd just taken a big bite of lemon. Compared to Amy's lethargic bay, Isolde was basically prancing.

"Is he okay?" Presley asked, not sure what to do to help.

"He will be," Harper said, frustration gritting her

voice. "Do you think you can hold Isolde? It's hard to cool him off and keep her from acting out at the same time."

"Do I need a helmet?" Presley asked, eyeing the energetic mare anxiously. After searching for statistics that could assuage her mom's fears, she was well aware that horse-related injuries could happen just as easily on the ground as they could in the saddle.

"Good point," Harper said, pausing to unbuckle her helmet and handing it to Presley. "See the dial on the back? If you twist that it should give you a little more room for your hair. It won't be perfect, but it'll work."

Presley crammed the helmet onto her head, buckled it under her chin, and took Isolde's reins from her friend.

"I've got to walk Zodiac until he cools down and stops breathing so hard so that he doesn't get tied up," Harper told her. "Would you feel comfortable getting Isolde untacked, or do you want to walk her with us?"

"I'll walk with you," Presley said, as much because she wasn't really sure she knew where to start untacking Isolde as because she wanted to understand what had just happened.

But Harper was clearly fuming, so instead of getting right to the point, Presley took the long way round.

"Zodiac?" she asked. "What kind of name is that?"

"His registered name is Codebreaker," Harper told her. "His last owner thought that Zodiac, like the Zodiac Killer, was a funny barn name."

"Dark," Presley said with a touch of admiration. She lowered the register of her voice for a mock-evil adult accent, "Ah, yes, may I introduce you to my horse, Joseph Stallion, dictator of all horses. He may have replaced all of the barns with gulags, but it is for our own good!"

"You sound like Mrs. Roberts talking about the Soviet Union in history last week," Harper said.

"I bet Mrs. Roberts knows who the real Zodiac Killer was," Presley said, trying to distract her worried friend. "She seems like the red-string-covered-corkboard type."

Harper chuckled grimly, studying Zodiac. "This guy's last owner might have had a twisted sense of humor, but they wouldn't have done this to Zodiac."

"Letting someone else worry about him?" Presley asked, setting her jokes aside.

"If you don't cool horses down properly, they can get badly hurt or even die. Amy was being really irresponsible getting off and leaving him in this condition," Harper told her.

"I've read you need to walk them for a while to let them cool down, but I didn't know it was that big of a deal," Presley said. "What would have happened if you hadn't been here?"

Harper shrugged. "Amy would've found someone else to do this for her. She pulled stuff like this at our old barn all the time. Just because someone has a horse doesn't mean that they care about it or know how to take care of it."

"Aren't you mad that you don't get to ride now?" Presley asked.

"I guess. But I'd rather make sure Zodiac gets taken care of than get time in the saddle," Harper told her. "After all, we can't ride at all if our horses are lame or sick, right? And even though I could not possibly care less if Amy ever rides again, I do care that Zodiac gets to jump again. This horse *loves* to jump."

"You're really different than I thought you were," Presley blurted out.

Harper looked at her, confused, and Presley instantly regretted what she'd said.

"I don't mean in a bad way," Presley said, talking more to fill the awkward space between them than to get a point across. "You're great. I just meant . . ."

"You thought I was a snob," Harper said with a laugh.

"I thought you were like Amy," Presley said sheepishly.

"Ewwwwww," Harper moaned. Then she punched Presley's arm lightly. "Take it back."

"I take it back!" Presley affirmed. "You're nothing like Amy."

"Thanks," Harper said, and paused, sticking her hand into Zodiac's armpit—or whatever word there was to describe a horse's armpit. "He's a lot cooler now. It's probably safe to untack him."

With Harper's careful supervision, Presley untacked Isolde while her friend took care of Zodiac. They'd just finished hosing the horses off when Harper's mom appeared in the barn aisle.

"Almost done?" she asked Harper.

"Almost. Sorry, Mom," Harper said. And with a conspiratorial smile at Presley, she offered an explanation. "Barn time."

The girls were still giggling when they pulled out of the barn's driveway a few minutes later. Presley was already counting the hours until she got to come back tomorrow.

Chapter Thirteen

"I'm nervous about my lesson this weekend," Presley admitted to Harper. They were waiting outside the middle school for Mahal to pick them up and take them to the barn.

"What are you nervous about?" Harper asked. "You're getting so much more comfortable around Isolde, and you've only been to the barn three times."

Presley hadn't told her friend what Amy had said about her. There wasn't a point, after all. Harper couldn't make Amy treat Presley kindly any more than she could make her take good care of her horse. But Amy's words had eaten away at her. What if she *was* starting too late? What if she got on and realized that the dream she'd held so tightly since she was a little kid was impossible? What if she hated it?

Worst of all, Presley's mom was coming to watch her lesson, and Presley was becoming more and more afraid of getting hurt, especially right in front of her mom. If something happened to her, that was it. Presley would never set foot near a horse again. The thought had kept her up late the night before, scrolling the internet for something that would make her feel better.

She hadn't found it. If Harper could see her internet search history and all the horrifying stories Presley had read with one eye open late at a night, Harper would be afraid too. And that was the worst part—it was like Mom's worry had taken over her brain and was slowly scraping away any excitement that Presley had ever had about riding. The dream of effortless and magical connection between Presley and a horse had swapped places with her mom's flimsy what-if scenarios. Reality seemed to be siding with the no-nonsense consequences of the adult world in a way that made Presley's old vision about riding horses feel like the kind of dream she could barely remember after waking up. Tracie had been lucky to get out of her accident with a few broken bones, Presley thought. It could have been so much worse.

When Presley didn't say anything, Harper pressed. "Would it help if you got to know the horse you were going to be riding?"

Presley looked up at her, curious. "How would I find that out?"

"We'll ask Tracie, silly," Harper said. "After we do stalls and whatever else Tracie has for us today, we can spend some time with the horse you're going to ride. So long as they're not in a lesson. I can show you some of the groundwork basics that we use to teach horses manners. That way you'll be more comfortable on Saturday."

"But don't you want to ride?" Presley asked.

"It's Isolde's day off," Harper told her. "Marnie had a lesson on her yesterday, and my lesson is tomorrow."

"What about Penelope?"

"I promise you that showing you how to do some groundwork would be way more fun than convincing Penelope to leave her hay net."

Just then, Mahal pulled up, and the girls hopped into the back seat. After they'd said hello and answered the usual questions about what they learned in school, Harper picked up right where she'd left off.

"Some of the lesson horses know some really cool tricks. Rory can fist-bump and smile, Lemon knows how to fetch, and Rigo does all of that, plus he bows and gives kisses," Harper said with a smile.

"I've been around enough horse slobber to know

that the last thing I want is a kiss from a horse," Mahal piped up.

"Ew," the girls said in unison.

"That's nothing. Want to hear what I got to pull out of a dalmatian's guts in surgery today?"

Presley covered her face with her hands and groaned. "Not everyone has the stomach for surgery stories, Mahal."

"I do!" Harper exclaimed. "Tell me *everything*."

Mahal trotted out his goriest, grossest, and most gruesome stories of veterinary surgery for the rest of the drive to the barn. And, much to Presley's delight and surprise, Harper had as much of an appetite for Mahal's stories as she did. More, even. Presley didn't like hearing about the times when Mahal almost lost patients, even though the sad moments were as much of a part of his job as the successes. Harper, on the other hand, seemed to innately understand and appreciate how fragile animal lives were, and she wasn't at all squeamish about it.

When Mahal stopped the car in front of the big green barn, he twisted around and fixed his eyes on Presley. "I want you to remember three things while you're here, okay, kiddo?"

"What?" Presley asked, eyeing Harper perched

on the seat next to her with her hand on the door handle.

"I want you to try to stay in the present, okay? No thinking ten steps ahead. That's how you get hurt, and your mom will murder me and turn me into the Sunday dinner special if you get hurt. She thinks I'm the one who opened the door for all this in the first place, after all."

Harper giggled at that, but Presley knew that under his dark jokes, Mahal was serious. And something about him acknowledging that this thing she wanted to do so badly was dangerous made her feel just a little bit braver.

"Second, listen to everything Tracie says, and follow all her rules to the letter."

"Done," the girls said in unison. Presley didn't need to spend a lot of time in Tracie's barn to know that it was her way or the highway. And she was not about to lose this opportunity.

"Third," Mahal said, taking his glasses off, and pointing them at the girls to emphasize his point. "Be safe and have fun."

"That's two rules," Presley pointed out.

"It's not," Mahal countered. "Being safe is *how* you have fun. Got it?"

Presley and Harper nodded, bouncing in their seats and waiting for Mahal to let them loose.

"Okay. I'll be back to get you in a few hours. Be good."

The last word was barely out of his mouth before Harper and Presley were out of the car and booking it into the barn. They didn't have a moment to spare, after all, if they were going to get through the tasks Tracie had assigned them with enough time to do anything fun.

Together, Harper and Presley mucked stalls, swept the barn aisle, reorganized the saddle pads, and cleaned four saddles in record time. Other riders greeted them and stopped to chat briefly as they went about their own tasks to take care of their horses before or after their rides. Some even offered to help. And Harper told Presley about each and every one of them. Tracie's barn was home to everyone from amateur adults who'd been riding and competing their whole lives to kids who were barely big enough to take lunge-line lessons on Tracie's littlest pony.

But what stood out to Presley the most was that all of them—with the glaring exception of Amy—were kind, welcoming, and encouraging.

When they were finally finished with their chores,

Harper led Presley over to the barn's office door and knocked softly. Tracie told them to come in a second later. Tinny hold music came from the cell phone sitting on her desk on speaker mode, and Tracie stared fixedly at her computer screen while she used a pencil to scratch the inside of her wrist that was stuck in a cast. Harper waited a second, but when Tracie didn't look up, she cleared her throat.

"Uh, Tracie?" Harper asked. "Presley and I were wondering if we might be able to do a little get-to-know-you groundwork session with whoever Presley's going to be riding on Saturday."

"Is that okay?" Presley added. "We don't want to be a bother."

Tracie looked up at them blankly for a few seconds, blinked a couple of times, and then glanced over at the whiteboard calendar on the wall. "Of course. I'm going to start you on Rigo, Presley. He's down in the back left pond paddock with Rush, Bill, and Steward. Where are you going to work, Harper?"

"Round pen?" Harper asked.

She nodded briskly. Just then, a disembodied voice trembled over the line. "Ms. McLaughlin? Are you there?"

Tracie picked up the phone and held up a hand.

"Yes. Just one second, okay?" she said into the phone, then looked at the girls. "No cookies for Rigo, okay? If you want to give him snacks, there are hay pellets in the feed room and watermelon rinds in the fridge in the lounge."

Turning her attention back to her phone, Tracie waved Harper and Presley out of her office. The girls exchanged identical looks of excitement and broke several world records for fastest power walk as they zoomed off toward the lounge.

Chapter Fourteen

"Watermelon *rinds*?" Presley asked after following her friend into the lounge.

"Rinds," Harper confirmed. "They're low sugar, which is good for greedy old ponies like Rigo. Some horses don't like them, but Rigo likes *everything*. And I love him. You will too."

Treats acquired, Presley and Harper walked down the quiet, grassy lane between the paddocks, stopping at each one so that Harper could introduce Presley to the horses. They came in all colors, shapes, and sizes—from enormous draft horses to tiny miniature horses—and it seemed like Windy Creek welcomed every horse with the same spirit of generosity and openness that it had shown Presley. And even though Harper and Marnie had only moved their horses to Windy Creek a few months ago, Harper seemed to know everything about every single animal on the property.

"How do you remember so much?" Presley asked.

"Says the girl with, what was it? Thirty-seven pets?" Harper said laughing. "They're just like people. You get to know their personalities and quirks a little, and you remember them."

"Just two cats, a dog, a snake, two lizards, and fifteen birds," Presley corrected her friend with a smile. "I see what you mean."

Harper stopped beside a gate and sorted through the halters hanging there. She picked out a bright green one and held it up for Presley to see. *RIGO* was written in Sharpie on the nylon.

"All of Tracie's horses' halters are labeled like this. Some of them have fancy leather halters, but she doesn't leave those out to get rained on. And if you can't find the halter for the horse you're looking for, all you have to do is ask," Harper told her.

"Do you ever get embarrassed about asking questions? I feel like I'm never going to catch up, and everyone knows so much more than I do," Presley confessed, following Harper into the field.

"Marnie always says it's better to ask questions than do something that might get me or one of the horses hurt," Harper said. "Plus, no one around here's going to judge you."

Presley closed and latched the gate carefully behind them and muttered, "Except Amy."

"You know why I don't worry about Amy?" Harper asked.

Presley shook her head.

"Because I know that even though she always has the fanciest tack and riding clothes and even the nicest horses, she doesn't love riding the same way I do. She might even win blue ribbons and trophies, but she's never going to have the kind of relationship with Zodiac that I do with Penelope or Isolde, even though we just bought her. She doesn't spend time with her horse, and she doesn't care about horsemanship as much as she does about winning." Harper flipped her ponytail over her shoulder and squinted out over the rolling green hills. "Now let's stop talking about Amy and find Rigo."

It took some doing, but they finally spotted Rigo standing in the farthest corner of the field with his field mates. He was a squat, brown-and-white pinto pony with a wildly thick, fluffy mane and tail.

"Do you want to put his halter on him, or do you want me to show you?" Harper asked.

Presley felt the nervous bubble of worry trembling in her stomach like a bowl of Jell-O, but she forged ahead, taking the halter Harper offered her. "Just slip it over his head and buckle it under his chin, right?" she asked, looking for reassurance.

Smiling, Harper nodded. Presley approached Rigo, who seemed way more interested in the patch of grass he was eating than in the girls. Presley waited a minute for him to lift his head so she could put his halter on, but he just kept eating. She glanced over at Harper helplessly.

"How do I make him put his head up?" she asked.

Harper shook her head woefully. "What a stubborn little man," she admonished the pony. "Try looping his lead rope around his neck and using that to gently pull his head up. I can help if you want it."

"Let me try," Presley said, and as soon as she tugged lightly on the loop of lead rope, Rigo lifted his head and started sniffing Presley's pockets, looking for treats. Presley couldn't help but grin. She was doing it!

As she was buckling his halter, she noticed that one of his eyes was a cloudy, dark gray color. "Is something going on with his eye?" Presley asked. "I could get Mahal to look at it."

"He's blind in his left eye. See?" Harper said, waving her hand in front of the cloudy eye.

"Does it bother him?" Presley asked.

"Not a bit," Harper told her. "He's mostly bomb-proof. You could literally set off fireworks from his back and he wouldn't blink an eye."

Presley giggled.

"Not that I suggest trying that," Harper added quickly. "All of the other horses would freak out, and you never know when a horse might spook. They are prey animals, after all."

"Harper Lawrence! What about me makes you think you needed to clarify that?" Presley asked with a mischievous grin.

With Harper watching over her carefully, Presley led Rigo up the lane and into the round pen. Harper latched the gate behind them and set her dressage whip and the plastic container of watermelon rinds on the mounting block just outside the pen. Rigo nosed around Presley's pockets, searching for a treat, and Presley scratched the top of his head between his ears, waiting for Harper to tell her what to do next. She had absolutely no idea where to start.

"You already have the basics of leading a horse," Harper said. "You proved that the other day when you led Isolde for me. You didn't even have to think about it."

Harper was right, Presley realized. She'd just led

the horse by instinct. She'd been too upset by Amy's neglect of her horse to feel nervous or doubt herself.

"Horses can tell how we're feeling," Harper reminded her. "So any time you're trying to tell a horse what you want them to do, you have to do it confidently. Even if you get the cue wrong, so long as you believe in yourself, the worst they'll think is that they don't know what you're asking for."

Presley's slightly faded dream flared a little more brightly with Harper's reminder. Horses were special creatures and she could form a bond and communicate with them if she worked hard enough.

First, Harper showed Presley how to ask Rigo to back up, which was easy. She just put a little pressure backward on the lead rope and said, "Back," and Rigo took several steps backward. When she was confident making him go forward and backward, Harper showed her how to face his hind end and ask him to turn on the forehand—move his back legs away from her in a circle without moving his front legs. It didn't take long at all for Presley to get that down pat.

Every time Rigo did what she asked, she felt a little steadier, and a little less afraid. Rigo wasn't nearly as big as Isolde or Zodiac and he was absolutely dwarfed by the draft horses who were watching them

curiously from their nearby paddock. But he was still a whole lot bigger than any of the animals Presley had at home, and *way* bigger than she was. If Rigo wanted to hurt her, he for sure could. But Presley felt more and more certain that this little pony didn't have a mean bone in his body, and she very much believed that was true about all of the horses at Windy Creek—and horses in general.

"How do I get him to bow?" Presley asked eagerly after giving the pony a watermelon rind reward for turning on his haunches—moving his front end around in a circle like his back legs were the sun and his front legs were planets in orbit around it.

Grinning, Harper held her hands out for the lead rope and dressage whip. Presley handed them over and climbed up to perch on the top of the fence to get out of the way. Harper unclipped Rigo's lead rope and sent him out to trot along the edge of the round pen with a flick of the whip and a chirping, "Teeee-rot!"

When he'd done three full rotations of the pen, Harper said, "Rigo! Right!" And pointed to her right. Rigo quickly changed direction and kept trotting. After a few rounds, Harper said, "Rigo! Here!"

Rigo came to a halt in front of Harper and looked at her, waiting for his next cue or, maybe more accurately, for these kids to be done with him so he could go back to snacking with his friends in the field. With a flourish, Harper bowed to Rigo and said, "Rigo! Bow!"

Just like that, Rigo tucked his right front hoof up close to his chest and sank back and down until his right knee was nearly touching the sandy footing of the round pen. Presley's dream grew more solid in her heart, and her mother's world of fear and consequences seemed further away than it had since she first came to the barn. Delighted, Presley burst into applause. That startled the little pony, and he took off at an (admittedly slow) canter around the round pen.

"I'm sorry!" Presley exclaimed, hopping down off the fence to help Harper catch Rigo.

Presley apologized again as they steadied Rigo with lots of neck scratches and watermelon rinds, and once he was standing placidly next to them with one hoof cocked and a sleepy, half-lidded expression in his one seeing eye, Presley said, "I'm really sorry. That could have been dangerous."

Harper looked up at her, and Presley was surprised to find that she didn't look irritated at all. "It's okay, Presley. Seriously. No one got hurt. And even if one of us had, it wouldn't have been your fault. Horses spook, and you didn't know that Rigo hates the sound of clapping. I should have told you. But now you know. No harm done, right?"

Presley nodded. "Right."

"Now, are you going to take a turn making him bow, or are you going to let him get away with thinking that all he has to do is spook to get out of work?" Harper asked.

"I'll try," Presley said. "But do I have to bow for him to do it too?"

"Nope! I just think it's fun and it makes the whole thing look way cooler."

Presley did too. It took her a few tries—Harper said that Rigo wasn't entirely convinced that Presley was the boss of him yet—but eventually, she got Rigo to bow for her. By the time Mahal came to pick them up, Harper had taught Presley how to ask Rigo for all his tricks, and she was a lot more comfortable around the stubborn little pony. She couldn't wait for her lesson.

Chapter Fifteen

Presley sprang awake a full half hour before her alarm went off the morning of her lesson. Certain that she'd slept through it, she grabbed her cell phone from her nightstand to check the time and lay back into the pillow with a sigh. All night long she'd had nightmares about giant hands springing out of the sandy arena flooring and clapping loudly to spook Rigo, and the letters around the arena transforming into knights set on attacking her. She was more than a little nervous. That was for sure.

But she was also so, so excited. She'd never thought that Mom would change her mind—not about horses—but here she was, about to take her first ever riding lesson. And Mom wasn't just coming, she'd gotten one of her kitchen managers to cover the Saturday morning lunch rush *and* the weekly farmer's market run. Mom never, ever let anyone else go to the farmer's market to pick out produce for the restaurant. Presley wasn't going to let her feel like she'd wasted her time.

She had laid out her clothes the night before, but since she'd woken up so early, Presley took her time getting dressed. The breeches Harper had found for her in the free bin at the barn were the same boring tan that she'd seen on every other rider there, and the tall boots, despite being lovely, soft leather, were plain black and just as boring as the breeches. Presley decided to bring some life to the outfit with one of her favorite T-shirts.

By the time she was dressed, Presley could hear her family's chaos coming to life throughout the house below her. Ahmed and Kierkegaard thundered up and down the stairs creating more noise than physics should have allowed, the cats yowled for their breakfasts, and Mom was unloading the dishwasher with a vigor and decibel level she reserved for weekend mornings. Presley reached down to grab her boots and realized that her hands were shaking.

What if something happens to me? she wondered. *What if I fall off and Mom never lets me anywhere near a horse for the rest of my life? What if I get hurt?*

Her busy mind had no trouble coming up with all

the ways the day might go wrong. But instead of letting those thoughts run away with her like a wild mustang, Presley took a deep breath, just like her dad always told her to when she was upset, and looked at the facts. She'd already learned so much more being around horses at Windy Creek than she ever could have gotten from a book. She'd led Isolde and gotten Rigo to do tricks. And when she wasn't worrying, she was actually pretty good at it. "A natural," like Harper said all the time. Plus, Tracie would be there, and Presley knew that she would do her very best to keep Presley safe.

Already starting to feel better, Presley grabbed the helmet she'd borrowed from the barn and headed downstairs. She had chores to do before her lesson, and she smelled bacon. She'd have to get the chickens fed and the cat boxes cleaned *fast* if she wanted a plate before her siblings devoured every last bite.

She set her boots and helmet carefully by the front door, slid on a pair of Crocs, and went to grab a piece of bacon on the way to do her chores. But she stopped short at the kitchen door. A package wrapped in rainbow paper waited for her in her usual chair.

Seeing her in the doorway, Mom wiped her hands on the kitchen towel draped over her shoulder and held out her arms. "Mahal's taking care of your chores this morning," Mom said as Presley hugged her. "It's a big day for you. How are you feeling?"

"Nervous," Presley admitted.

"You're nervous?" Mom asked laughing. "That must make me somewhere on the road to a breakdown."

"Everything is going to be just fine," Mahal said, coming in from the backyard. "Presley is great with animals, and Tracie promised you how many times that she'd take good care of her?"

"Just because Tracie promised doesn't mean—"

Mahal cut Mom off with a smile and a finger to his lips. "She's going to be okay, my love."

"Who's the present for?" Ahmed asked as he plucked a piece of bacon off the plate by the stove.

"Whose chair is it in?" Rishi asked exasperatedly, following him into the kitchen. "Pres, you okay if I don't come today? I have a physics project due on Monday."

Presley made a face. She'd accepted the fact that her mom was going to watch. She even kind of appreciated it. Mom had come a long way from never wanting Presley to set foot in a barn to showing up for her first lesson. But that didn't mean that she wanted the rest of her family to come too.

She said, "Please don't! I don't need an audience."

At the same time, Mom said, "Your project can wait. This is important to your sister."

Rishi looked to Mahal to come down on one side or the other.

"I promised Fred I would FaceTime him so that he could watch," Mahal said. "That's all I know."

Fred—Presley's dad—was a filmmaker and often away on set. That month he was shooting a documentary in Germany. A lot of her friends with divorced parents thought it was weird that all her parents got along, but Presley kind of loved it. Most of the time.

"You go to all of your siblings' sports games and concerts," Mom said to Presley. "It's only fair that they come watch you ride."

"Ew," Presley said with a shudder. "What if they come to my first horse show instead of my first lesson? I hate watching them practice. They shouldn't have to watch my lessons."

"Can't argue with that," Gabe said from the doorway. "When's breakfast?"

"After your sister opens her present," Mom said, frowning at him.

"You guys didn't have to get me anything," Presley said. "You're already giving me the thing I want the most in the world."

"Do I get a present too?" Ahmed asked.

Presley smiled at her younger brother, who was feeding a piece of pancake to their greyhound, Kierkegaard, as if he hadn't been told a thousand times not to feed the dog at the table.

"Your birthday was last month," Gabe said, grabbing a pancake from the platter in the center of the kitchen table. "Didn't get enough presents then?"

Ahmed stuck his tongue out at Gabe, and Mom waved Presley toward the table.

"Open your present," she said. "We're going to be late for your lesson if we don't get going soon, and I'm not bringing you to Tracie with an empty stomach."

Presley didn't think her nervous stomach could handle much breakfast, but she knew better than to argue with her mom about food, so she began carefully opening the present.

"You're not going to reuse the wrapping paper," Rishi scolded. "Just rip it open."

"Yeah!" Ahmed joined in. "Rip it!"

Ignoring them, Presley got the wrapping paper off in one clean piece. She might not wrap anything with it, but it was still good for crafts, after all. Presley didn't waste things if she didn't have to. She lifted the lid and gasped. Beneath the tissue paper, a brand-new helmet waited for her atop a pile of breeches in all the colors of the rainbow.

"All of this is for me?" Presley asked in shock.

"I don't think that you could have chosen a sport with more gear," Mahal said. "The least we could do was get you a few things that felt a little more like *you* than those boring old tan breeches."

Presley set the box carefully back in the chair and launched herself at her parents, hugging them hard.

"Thank you," she said. "Thank you so much."

"Be sure to thank your dad and stepmom too. They helped out," Mom said. "Now eat your breakfast and get changed. Seat belts buckled in fifteen."

Chapter Sixteen

Harper was waiting outside when Presley's parents' station wagon stopped in front of Windy Creek Stables' big green barn. She was grinning from ear to ear and almost bouncing out of her boots. Presley had barely opened the car door before she started talking.

"I picked out the perfect saddle pad for you," Harper said without preamble.

Presley's mom, who'd insisted that she couldn't show up to the barn empty-handed, grabbed a basket bursting with sandwiches made with leftover pancakes stuffed with bacon and extra-sharp cheddar cheese from the trunk and fixed Harper with an expectant smile.

"Harper, I assume?"

"Yes, ma'am. Sorry, ma'am," Harper and Presley said in unison.

"Maybe you can point me in Tracie's direction before you get started?" Mom asked.

"I'll show you the way," Mahal said. Rishi and Gabe had offered to watch Ahmed during Presley's lesson, and, much to Presley's relief, Mom and Mahal had agreed. Having Mom and Mahal there and Dad watching through Mahal's phone was enough pressure. She didn't need her siblings there too.

"I already told Tracie that I would help get Presley ready for her lesson," Harper said. "Mine is this afternoon, but Mom dropped me off early. I didn't want to miss it!"

When Mom and Mahal were safely out of earshot, Presley turned to her friend and held out a shaking hand. "Is it normal to be this nervous?" she asked.

"Of course," Harper said. "I threw up before my first show. Maybe that was all the cotton candy or maybe it was nerves. Either way, it was gross. Nice breeches, by the way."

"Thanks. They're new," Presley said. She had chosen a pair of sky-blue breeches from the bounty that she'd been given that morning. Pastels weren't really her usual style, but these breeches felt like a good compromise between the boring tan ones that seemed to be the standard and the bright colors she preferred. They made her feel polished and cool. Plus, they matched her hair.

"Rigo's in his stall. Want to go get him and get tacked up?" Harper asked.

"If you promise to make sure I don't mess up!" Presley countered.

"Promise," Harper said. "You don't have to worry. I'll double-check your tack and so will Tracie. Plus, Rigo's basically bombproof, remember? He's going to take such good care of you."

Presley buckled her new helmet snugly onto her head, took Rigo's reins from Harper, and led the little pinto pony down the ramp and into the arena. Tracie was waiting for her there with a big smile plastered on her face. Presley glanced over and saw her mom sitting right up next to the rail on the observation deck. Mahal, holding up his phone with one hand, waved at her with the other. Presley took a deep breath, wishing she could have a long, firmly worded talk with the butterflies in her stomach.

"Ready to go?" Tracie asked.

Presley nodded.

"Okay. There are few things that we check every time we get on. First, I want you to check your girth. Some horses will tense up when you tighten the girth, and even if they don't, it's a good idea to make sure it's nice and snug before you get on."

Tracie lifted the saddle flap and gave the girth a tug, tightening it one extra hole on each strap.

"Next, we're going to adjust your stirrups. Did Harper already show you how?" Tracie asked.

"No, ma'am," Presley answered, hearing her voice tremble as she got closer and closer to *actually riding*.

"No problem," Tracie said. "It's not exact, but if you put the metal end of the stirrup, where your foot goes, right up into your armpit and hold your arm out straight with your fingertips touching the saddle, that's *about* how long you want your stirrups to be. We'll adjust them more once you're in the saddle, but when you're riding lesson horses, someone else has probably ridden your horse in their saddle that week, so make sure to check before you try to mount."

Presley paid close attention while Tracie inspected every piece of tack from Rigo's nose to his tail, even picking up his feet to make sure Presley and Harper had picked them out carefully. Tracie's attention to detail and explanations made Presley feel a little less nervous. Tracie walked beside Presley as she led Rigo over to the mounting block, where she took the reins from Presley and looped them over his neck.

"What do I do now?" Presley asked, furrowing her brows. It felt like such a simple thing—just mount up, right? But Presley realized she had no idea where to start.

Tracie, holding the reins with one hand, gestured to the mounting block with her arm in its cast. "Step up to the top of the mounting block, then put one hand on the pommel—that's—"

"The front of the saddle," Presley cut in.

"Right," Tracie agreed. "And the other on the cantle—the back."

Presley did as she was told, thinking about how she knew that you mounted a horse from the left side because back in the day, that kept people from getting tangled up in their swords or spears when they were mounting up. But she didn't know how to get her body up and into the saddle. Tracie told her to put her left foot in the stirrup and swing her right leg over Rigo's back. Presley slipped her foot into the metal stirrup, and suddenly felt her legs starting to shake.

"I'm nervous," she admitted, quietly enough that only Tracie could hear her.

"It would be weird if you weren't. But I won't let anything happen to you," Tracie assured her in a quiet voice, and looked down to her hand on the reins. "Don't worry about Rigo. He'll stand here as long as we let him. Take your time, and when you're ready, just step up into the stirrup like you're walking up a set of stairs. You can throw your whole body across the saddle too if it feels weird to balance on one foot."

Presley took her foot back out of the stirrup and leaned over, putting her tummy on the saddle just to see how it felt. Rigo didn't move a muscle, which helped steady Presley's nerves enough that she decided to go for it. She put her left foot in the stirrup and stepped up.

It was *nothing* like going up stairs. The stirrup wobbled, and Presley grabbed a handful of Rigo's mane so that she wouldn't fall. It was awkward and weird, but Presley managed to scramble into the saddle. She sat up straight and took a deep breath. She'd done it. She was riding a horse!

Even though Rigo was just 13.3 hands high—just over four feet tall at his withers—Presley felt like she was sitting on top of a mountain. Tracie adjusted Presley's stirrups again and helped her balance her weight in the saddle. When she was settled, Presley looked over at Tracie, waiting expectantly.

"Now what?" she asked.

"I'm going to clip a lunge line to Rigo's bridle," Tracie said. "He's a good pony, but the lunge line is kind of a safety net for you while you get comfortable riding."

"So it's for babies," Presley said, feeling a little dejected. She *knew* she was a beginner, but she didn't like *feeling* like she didn't know what she was doing.

Tracie laughed. "Not at all. I still take lunge lessons from time to time. It just lets you focus on *you*, not Rigo. And everyone needs to focus on themselves when they first start riding."

That made Presley feel a little better. While Tracie got her equipment sorted, Presley focused on trying to make her body do the things that she'd read about for years. She pushed her weight down into her heels and turned her toes in toward Rigo's body, feeling burning protest in her calf muscles and hips. After years of pretending with belts and pieces of string, Presley thought that the reins would feel comfortable threaded between her ring finger and pinkie and looped back over her hand, but the leather was both too thick and too wide at the same time.

"Good position," Tracie complimented, taking a step back and assessing Presley. "In a second you're going to ask Rigo to walk forward, but first we're going to practice the most important thing a rider can learn."

"What's that?" Presley asked.

"Whoa," Tracie and Harper said simultaneously.

Presley grinned over at her friend, watching from the side of the arena in front of the observation deck.

"I think I know how to do that," Presley said.

"Explain it to me," Tracie said with an encouraging smile.

"If I want a horse to stop, I need to stop moving with his rhythm, sit deep into the saddle, breathe in, and say whoa. Then, if he's not listening, use the reins to pull back as lightly as I can. As soon as he stops, I give him his head. Right?"

"Perfect," Tracie said. "Do you have any questions?"

"Just, uh, let me know if I'm doing it right, I guess," Presley said.

Harper giggled, and Tracie said, "That's my whole job, kiddo. Okay, I want you to ask Rigo to walk. Sit up straight, put your weight into your heels, and squeeze Rigo's barrel with your calves."

Concentrating, Presley did as she was told, and Rigo stepped forward into a walk. Joy bubbled up in

Presley's stomach like soda spilling out of a shaken can. She hadn't thought that she would ever get to do this, and here she was. Riding a horse. It was perfect.

After Rigo and Presley completed a few laps around Tracie on the lunge line at the walk, asking Rigo to stop every few steps, and making tiny adjustments to the way she was moving and holding her body according to Tracie's instructions, Presley was already feeling more confident. Sitting on Rigo's back had felt so strange and high off the ground at first, but after just a few minutes, the strangeness disappeared. It felt natural. Like Presley had finally found her place in the world.

"Do you feel like trying the trot?" Tracie asked.

Giddy, Presley nodded. "Yes, ma'am."

"Okay, so when we're riding the trot, most of the time we make it more comfortable for us and our horses by posting. Do you know what posting is?" Tracie asked.

Presley bit the inside of her cheek as she nodded. Of course she knew what posting was. She'd read every book in the library about horses, after all. But then she reminded herself that this was her first lesson, and that was almost all Tracie knew about her.

She was never going to learn if she couldn't remember that she was a beginner, and she was learning from Tracie for a reason.

"It's rising in the saddle to the beat of the gait," she recited from memory. "You rise when the outside front leg goes forward, right?"

"Perfect," Tracie congratulated her. "It's going to feel really weird and unnatural, but you kind of let the horse push you up and out of the saddle. Now, because Rigo is a pony and his legs are short, his trot feels really quick. That's okay. Just remember to keep your heels down and move with him. Whenever you're ready, squeeze him a little with your calves again to ask him to trot."

Tracie was right. Compared to his walk, Rigo's trot felt like riding a freight train. He was faster than a car. Faster than a racehorse. The little guy may have exceeded the speed of light, for all Presley knew. It was all Presley could do to stay on. After a few seconds of bouncing wildly, Tracie asked Rigo to whoa, and the pony calmly went back to his plodding walk.

"That was great," Tracie told Presley encouragingly.

"It was trash," Presley countered. "I feel like a freshly mixed can of paint."

That made Tracie laugh. "It wasn't trash. I promise.

We're going to try again in the other direction, and this time I want you to focus on breathing and moving with Rigo. Don't worry about the reins. Don't worry about his speed. Just think about putting your weight down in your heels and rising with his gait. It doesn't have to be much. Just sit up out of the saddle high enough that you could put a pancake between your butt and the saddle. Ready to try again?"

Presley imagined sitting on the stack of pancake sandwiches her mom had packed, and the ridiculous idea helped loosen her up a little. This time, it was a lot easier. She knew what to expect and she found Rigo's rhythm pretty quickly. After a few turns around Tracie, Presley was out of breath but smiling with everything in her. This was *fun*.

"I think you're ready to come off the lunge line," Tracie told Presley. She turned to look at the observation deck. "Mom, you okay with me taking Presley off the lunge line?"

Presley's mom held her worry furrowed between her eyebrows, but she said, "You're the expert."

Tracie gave Presley and her mom the same reassuring smile before unclipping the line and setting it in a neat coil on top of the mounting block. She instructed Presley to guide Rigo to the rail at the walk, taking her time to really feel how he reacted when she shifted her weight or moved the reins. Presley decided to try a whoa without Tracie on the other end of the lunge line. She sat deep, tightened her abs, and stopped moving with Rigo. He stopped immediately, without Presley having to touch the reins.

That gave her a lot of confidence, so when Tracie asked if she wanted to trot, Presley immediately nodded. Following Tracie's instructions, she tightened her reins by caterpillaring her fingers down the leather straps so that there was less distance between the bit in Rigo's mouth and her hands. She gave him a light squeeze, and they were off. Presley focused on remembering to breathe as she posted up and down along with Rigo's bouncy little gait. She was doing it! Until everything went wrong.

Chapter Seventeen

Applause erupted from the side of the arena. Rigo skittered to a stop. Presley's heart thundered in her chest as she grabbed at his fluffy mane. Panicking, she felt the little pony twist and buck beneath her. One second, she was in the saddle. The next, she was on her butt in the dirt, gasping for air.

Presley couldn't get a breath in: It felt like Rigo was sitting on her chest, that's how hard it was to breathe. And it *hurt*. Everything. She felt tears sting her eyes as the surprise and pain of falling washed over her.

Presley looked around wildly, statistics about injuries from falling off horses circling her head like tiny concussion birds in a cartoon. By the time she caught her breath, she saw that Rigo was nosing at a tuft of grass on the other side of the arena. After years of worrying about falling off a horse, Presley hadn't managed a whole hour on horseback before she fell. She didn't want to look over at her mom. Presley knew what she'd see on Mom's face. Presley was never going to be allowed to *look* at another horse.

Instead of facing her mom, Presley wiggled her toes. She could move them, which felt like a good sign. Inch by inch and joint by joint, Presley assessed herself. She didn't think she'd broken anything. In fact, nothing really hurt. Except her pride. It felt like an hour, but it couldn't have been more than a minute by the time Tracie was kneeling beside her.

"You okay?" Tracie asked.

Presley nodded.

"You have nothing to prove," Tracie reminded her. "It's okay if you don't want to get back on, for any reason. But if you're hurt, I need you to tell me."

"I'm okay," Presley said, surprised at the determination in her voice.

"Do you want to get back on or do you want to call it for today?" Tracie asked, glancing over her shoulder to the observation deck.

It was bad. Her mom was never going to let her anywhere *near* a horse again. Tears welled in her eyes, but Presley had put it off as long as she could. Fighting her tears away, Presley pasted a shaky smile on her face and looked up at her mom. She was standing frozen on the edge of the observation deck, jaw tight, and hands clenched around Mahal's arm. She looked terrified.

No. That wasn't it. Mom was *furious*.

In that moment Presley knew that if she didn't manage to get back in Rigo's saddle that day, her dream would be over. Between her fall and the cast on Tracie's wrist telling the story of her own accident, Presley's mom had all the facts that she would need to keep her off a horse for the rest of her life. Unless she could change Mom's mind.

But then she saw something else.

Amy. Her least favorite person at the barn was leaning against the wall on the ramp that led from the indoor arena to the barn. And she looked really, really pleased with herself.

She must have loved seeing Presley fall off. Determined not to lose her chance, Presley stood up, dusted herself off, and answered Tracie's question. "I want to get back on."

Harper, standing in the corner of the arena holding Rigo—who didn't look the least bit sorry for dumping Presley in the dirt—pumped her fist. "Yeah you will!" she called.

"You absolutely will not!" Mom said.

In a conspiratorial whisper, Tracie said, "Go get Rigo and bring him over to talk to your mom and me."

Presley did as she was told, and when she and Harper led Rigo over to the adults, she found them all talking over one another. She waited for an opening, and when she didn't find one, she looked to her dad, still on FaceTime with Mahal, for help. He put two fingers in his mouth and gave a shrill whistle, its volume tempered by the phone's tiny speakers.

"Look," Presley said, once the adults had quieted down. "I know why he spooked. Clapping scares him, right?"

Tracie nodded. "It's part of the reason he's in my lesson program and not a show pony anymore. I should have warned you, but it is *not* your fault."

Harper started to say something, but Mom interrupted her.

"We didn't clap," Mom said. "I could barely move!"

Harper squeezed Presley's hand and cleared her throat dramatically.

Tracie looked at her, one eyebrow raised. "Do you have something to say?"

"I saw who clapped," Harper said.

"Amy," Presley said, letting the name out slowly and quietly, like she was trying to see if it was true.

Tracie opened her mouth and then closed it, pressing her lips into a thin, tight line. "I'll deal with this. Wait just a minute."

With that, Tracie stomped out of the arena, and Harper and Presley exchanged wide-eyed looks.

From Mahal's phone, Dad asked, "Is everyone okay?"

"Amy may not be," Harper muttered.

Tracie came back a minute later, as the silence held between them was growing a little uncomfortable. "That won't be a problem again," she promised Presley's mom in a tone of voice that brooked no argument.

"I'm sorry," Presley said. "I should have kept my weight in my heels."

"It doesn't do any good to blame yourself for an accident. Especially with horses. You'll do better next time," Tracie said reassuringly, then turned her attention to Presley's parents. "Are you okay with her trying again? I can put her on the lunge line if that would make you feel better."

"Is the horse going to do that again?" Mom asked.

"Not unless you clap," Harper said.

Presley gave her friend a look that she hoped said to *be quiet*. Harper, understanding, pretended to zip her lips shut.

"You really want to try again?" Mom asked.

"More than anything," Presley assured her.

"I wouldn't offer to let her if I thought she was hurt," Tracie said. "Safety comes first at Windy Creek, and I know better than anyone not to get back on a horse if I'm hurt. But I also know that you can build a thing like this up in your head, and that can get in the way later. If you *can* get back on, it's always better to do that than to walk away and stew over it."

"Maybe next week we can practice falling?" Harper asked excitedly. "I love falling lessons."

Presley, seeing her mom's expression changing, looked at her Dad on FaceTime, begging him to step in.

"Let her try. Remember what we always say, Char. We can't protect our kids from failure. All we can do is teach them that it's okay to mess up so they learn how to handle challenges, right?" Dad said from Mahal's phone. "You've got this, kiddo."

That sealed it. Mom demanded a good long hug first, but Presley got back on Rigo and finished her lesson, grinning the whole time. When Tracie said it was time to get off, Presley had almost forgotten that she'd fallen in the first place.

"When can I come back?" she asked eagerly after she dismounted.

Tracie looked at Mom, questioning. Presley and Harper exchanged a nervous glance. Mom sighed, but rather than arguing, she said, "I want you to chase your dreams, Presley. I wouldn't be doing my job if I got in your way. When do you want to come back?"

Giddily, Presley handed Rigo's reins over to Harper and flung herself into her parents' arms. She'd won. She was going to be an equestrian.

Acknowledgments

This series wouldn't exist without Katherine Locke, and for their friendship, encouragement, and generosity, I will be forever grateful. Thank you for helping me find my way back to being a horse girl, and for always being there to commiserate over and celebrate the journey that is horsemanship.

I am also deeply grateful to my incredible agent, Molly Ker Hawn. Through many years, many manuscripts, and many hours of conversation you've made me a better writer and better person, and I am deeply grateful to be doing this with you. Thank you.

My incredible team at Feiwel & Friends has my eternal thanks for helping shape, improve, and bring this book to life. Thank you to my editor, Rachel Diebel, for seeing all the ways this book could be better and for enjoying the goofy jokes as much as I do. Mallory Grigg and Kelley McMorris have my eternal gratitude for packaging this story so beautifully; Linda

Minton deserves many thanks for fixing my negligent grammar and verifying all my horsey facts, Kelsey Marrujo and Leigh Ann Higgins for helping Presley and Harper find their readers. To everyone else whose names I have forgotten, I am so grateful for your hard work. Thank you.

I couldn't have done any of this publishing business without my friends and colleagues: Thalia Beaty, Dhonielle Clayton, Zoraida Cordova, Dana Decareaux, Tessa Gratton, Natalie C. Parker, Elissa Petruzzi, Ashley Poston, and Caroline Richmond. Thank you.

I am so lucky to have had the great privilege of learning from the people who've taught me (and let me ride their ponies) over the years: Stacey Adair, Leslie Wylie Bateman, Elizabeth Clifton, Sarah and Sandra Elder, Liz Green, Betsey Knight, Jamie Lawrence, Sarah Maurer, and Hailey Seals. Thank you. I have the best barn family in the whole world, and I'm so grateful for each and every one of you. And to all the horses who've stolen my heart: Farting Beauty, Riker, Miss City Kitty, Sailor, Henry, Rowdy, Raina, Q, Rory, and, of course, my sweet Boon: You are all so very loved.

My family: Thank you for believing in me and for encouraging me to get back on, even when it's scary.

Finally, I could not have done any of this without my husband. Cody, thank you for always saying yes to my harebrained schemes and all the creatures I bring into our home, for making me laugh, for giving me a reassure, for writing jokes for me, and for being the best partner a wild animal could ask for. I love you.

Thank you for reading this Feiwel & Friends book.
The friends who made

Windy Creek
⇾⇾⇾ Stables ⇽⇽⇽
Presley and the Impossible Dream

possible are:

Jean Feiwel, *Publisher*
Liz Szabla, *VP, Associate Publisher*
Rich Deas, *Senior Creative Director*
Anna Roberto, *Executive Editor*
Holly West, *Executive Editor*
Kat Brzozowski, *Senior Editor*
Dawn Ryan, *Executive Managing Editor*
Kim Waymer, *Senior Production Manager*
Emily Settle, *Editor*
Rachel Diebel, *Editor*
Foyinsi Adegbonmire, *Editor*
Brittany Groves, *Assistant Editor*
Mallory Grigg, *Senior Art Director*
Ilana Worrell, *Senior Production Editor*

Follow us on Facebook or visit us online at mackids.com. Our books are friends for life.